MW01615708

"Just when you thought the gay coming-out tale had exhausted itself, Steven Fales' solo show gives it a twist with the perspective of a Brokeback Mormon. But don't expect much rueful angst of a Western soul trying to resist what local folks can't abide. With a prepossessing smile, a musical-comedy persona, and the fervor of a proselyte on a decidedly different mission, Fales revels in his eventful autobiography while giving the audience . . . a glimpse into the mysterious intersection of faith and sexuality."

—*Variety*

"Who would have thought that the Mormon Church could be a perfect training ground for a life of prostitution? This being a fairly conventional, although admittedly compelling piece of confessional theater . . . there are eventually lessons to be learned . . . Mr. Fales learns to stop being a victim . . . carefully honed zingers . . . an appealing stage presence . . . his gleaming smile . . . and puffed-up muscles . . . giving his audience some beefcake. Say this for Fales: he knows how to sell it."

—*New York Times*

"Gay-themed monologues are hardly an endangered species around here . . . but Steven Fales' one-man show manages to inject some freshness to the genre. This colorful tale is related with much brio by Fales, who strips himself bare, both emotionally and physically, in the course of the evening. He's an engaging performer who's crafted his piece with an audience-pleasing sensibility. Fales' journey may have been a difficult one, but it sure makes for some great material."

—*NY Post*

"Fales' play is a gripping hybrid of memoir and theater . . . *Confessions* could have been maudlin and self-pitying but Fales sees the black comedy in his predicament and also allows us to share the rage he felt at the Catch-22 of being 'excommunicated for something that the Church said didn't exist.' *Mormon Boy* succeeds as non-fiction theater thanks to the writing and acting talent of a true survivor."

—*Connecticut Post*

"When Steven Fales gestures as if cradling a baby, the angle of his arms is so precise—and the expression so tender—you can tell he's cradled a real baby dozens of times. You can almost see the child in his arms—and its absence. For all its real pain, *Mormon Boy* delivers humor and considerable charm . . . it's a gem—funny, sad and illuminated by Fales' love for his children, his deep respect for Emily and his understanding of his motives and actions. It all leads up to a moment of vulnerability so simple and powerful, it suggests a kind of grace. All is forgiven with his final breathtaking, self-revelatory gesture. Fales describes his work as 'ultimately a prayer,' and at that moment, *Mormon Boy* makes you want to say 'amen.'"

—San Diego Union-Tribune

"The story couldn't be more timely. Affecting. Enlightening."

—San Francisco Chronicle

"A triumph! Shooting Latter-day Saints in a barrel might be satisfying to some know-it-all New Yorkers, but what elevates this autobiographical one-man show to the next level is that it probes deeper. Steven Fales is appealing from the beginning: a good-looking, well-built man with the smooth voice of a trained actor. Mormonism, he explains, teaches its followers to smile and press on despite the underlying pain, and Fales takes an analogous approach here. His intentions become clearer at the play's jolting climax, when the story takes a fascinating turn. Fales knows that the conflict in his life isn't just homosexuality versus Mormonism. As in all good theater, the protagonist must confront his own shortcomings and overcome them."

—Newsday

"Fales is taking audiences with him on a pendulum swing, from uncomfortable piety to uncontrolled sensuality, and finally to the stillness and peace of finding his authentic self. Tony Award-winning director Jack Hofsiss has helped sculpt the piece into something that's honest, moving, whimsical, sobering, tender, and cathartic. What works for him is something he finds only after exposing his soul and revealing his truths: He is, at last, comfortable in his own skin."

—Miami Herald

"The Smile charts Fales' internal Pilgrim's Progress . . . The play builds in power until it crests in a warm and satisfying wave that lifts theatergoers to their feet. As he comes to peace with himself, Fales provides a simple but startling coup de theatre to signal the emergence of the real human . . . his play shoots skyward in dramatic content and emotional payoff. In the end, *Confessions* is not about coping with a repressive world, but about getting past personal baggage and loving yourself."

—*South Florida Sun-Sentinel*

"The play is alternately funny and sad—and at its best moments, both . . . .a self-examination about accepting responsibility. Rather than blame his community or church, Fales sees his struggles as the result of his own obsessive desire to fit in and be accepted, whether by his Mormon 'brothers and sisters' or his wealthy tricks . . . honest and fascinating."

—*The Advocate*

"*Confessions* delivers true poignancy. Fales can be awfully funny, too. It is a balance of humor and pathos that is hard to achieve and even more difficult to sustain, and Fales succeeds. Rather than taking the easy route of attacking the Church, he castigates its leaders yet speaks of it with respect and even affection. Fales has crafted an absorbing tale that, in the end is less about a gay Mormon than about the universal human search for belonging. Mormon or not, gay or not, it's something we can all relate to . . . Feels like a sequel to *Good-bye, I Love You,* from the husband's perspective and a generation removed. An unflinchingly honest experience."

—*Salt Lake Tribune*

CONFESSIONS OF A
MORMON BOY

BEHIND THE SCENES OF THE
OFF-BROADWAY HIT

Steven Fales

FOREWORD BY TONY AWARD–WINNING
DIRECTOR OF *The Elephant Man*
JACK HOFSISS

This trade paperback original is published by Alyson Books,
P.O. Box 1253, Old Chelsea Station, New York, New York 10113-1251.

Distribution in the United Kingdom by Turnaround Publisher Services Ltd.,
Unit 3, Olympia Trading Estate, Coburg Road, Wood Green,
London N22 6TZ England.

ISBN-13 978-0-7394-7258-3

Front cover design by CH Major.
Front cover photographs by Dorothy Shi.
Book design by Victor Mingovits.

Contents

For "Buddy" and "Gee-Gee"

"If I were placed on a cannibal island and given the task of civilizing its people, I should straightaway build a theatre for the purpose. Upon the stage of the theater can be represented in character, evil and its consequences, good and its happy results and rewards; the weaknesses and the follies of man, the magnanimity of virtue and the greatness of truth. The stage can be made to aid the pulpit in impressing upon the minds of a community an enlightened sense of a virtuous life, also a proper horror of the enormity of sin and a just dread of its consequences. The path of sin with its thorns and pitfalls, its gins and snares can be revealed, and how to shun it."

—*Brigham Young*

Oh, when the saints go marching in,
Oh, when the saints go marching in,
Lord, how I want to be in that number.
When the saints go marching in

—*Old Gospel Spiritual*

Foreword by Jack Hofsiss

Anyplace. Two people. One speaks; one listens. Theatre at its most essential. Whether gathering around a campfire to hear those first stories centuries ago or gathering around the electric light of the most modern playhouse, it is theatre.

These thoughts were on my mind one summer afternoon not too long ago when, at the invitation of a producer, a young actor came to meet me to discuss my directing his play. As we went through the civilities of getting to know each other we discussed how best to talk about this play which I had not seen or read. Organically the actor began to speak the play to me. It was a solo piece, so it easily lent itself to this casual performance. It was anyplace (my living room), there was one person speaking (the storyteller) and one person listening (the audience). Without realizing it we were in the throes of a theatrical performance. This was my first experience of *Confessions of a Mormon Boy.*

As I worked with the playwright-actor on it over these last number of years, every production has been an attempt to capture for the audience the experience I had in my living room that day. This ferociously honest tale needs no excessive embellishment to make its powerful points. We all come from some community (religious or otherwise) with which we must make our peace as we gain our own beliefs and value systems. Steven's struggle to incorporate Mormonism into his life as a gay American is metaphoric for any journey to become whole with your traditions and faith. I have always been particularly struck by the play's refusal to disparage religion. Instead it speaks toward the inclusion of different sensibilities inside the whole.

This is a tale of faith, this is a tale of tradition, this is a tale of self-identification, this is a tale of love. Come gather around our literary campfire and hear this tale we tell.

Introduction

According to Mormon mythology, God has smiling, becoming children populating other worlds He has created all over the universe. Mormon founder Joseph Smith once taught that the Moon was populated by Mormons. (Not to be confused with the Moonies.) I've made it my personal mission to simply meet every gay Mormon on *this* planet. So far I'm making good progress. (And that doesn't necessarily mean I've slept with them all.) Wherever I perform *Confessions of a Mormon Boy*—from San Francisco to New York, Chicago to Miami—Lesbian Gay Bisexual Transgender Mormons seem to find me, sometimes flying thousands of miles. As long as good, upstanding, comely Mormon couples across the galaxy continue having babies, and the Church continues to condemn and reject its homosexual members throughout the universe, there will always be queer Mormons to shake hands with after the show.

Latter-day Q-Saints are everywhere. We've been around since the Church was founded in 1830. There are thousands upon thousands of us gay Mormons. Statistically, we are approaching a million throughout the world. Our stories are unique and yet the same—we are bonded by our colorful Mormon heritage and our diverse sexual orientations and circumstances. And I promise we are much more dimensional than anything you'll see in the recent gay films *Latter Days* or *Angels in America*, we give an entirely different spin to HBO's *Big Love*, and mainstream Mormons aren't all fundamentalist freaks you read about in the nonfiction bestseller *Under the Banner of Heaven*.

I think I speak for most when I say Mormons are hot! It is the consensus in the gay community that there are a disproportionate number of gay Mormons among us. All I have to do is wear a BYU T-shirt into a gay bar, LGBT Center, or Gay Pride event and I'll leave with three or four (or more!) new Mormon best friends for life. I've done it many times. Gays make great Mormons. Mormons make great gays. *"Oh, the Mormons and the Homos should be friends!"* (Just call me a "Momo-sexual.")

What is becoming evident to me is that my work doesn't just speak to Mormons or gays. As I've written specifically from my queer Mormon point of view, the play seems to be landing universally. It plays as well in Salt Lake City as it does in New York, though the themes and humor are sometimes appreciated differently. Salt Lake gets the religious and spiritual nuance of the first half. New York really gets the gritty urban underbelly of the second half. Other cities like Chicago and San Diego and Atlanta seem to get it all. There is apparently something for everyone.

As I greet the audience after every show or read their emails and letters, I get all kinds of comments—from gay, straight, male, female, old, young, religious, nonreligious—telling me how much the play means to them. "Did you steal my journals to write this play? I'm Lutheran!" or "You've told 99 percent of my story. I'm Jewish. Or Muslim!" or "I was excommunicated, too, and I'm straight!" or "Except for the escorting part, we have lived parallel lives!" or better yet "I was a sex worker too, and I grew up a good Catholic girl!" I'm realizing that this is not just my story of reclamation; it is many of our stories.

What we all seem to have in common is spiritual abuse. I define spiritual abuse as any time an individual or group uses religion to justify telling or showing anyone that he or she is not worthy of God's full love and blessings—including basic human rights. My excommunication from the church of my birth for the practice of homosexuality (in the twenty-first century!) is an overt form of spiritual abuse. Nothing would please me more than to see this medieval, barbaric cult tactic cease and desist in my lifetime. No one should be excommunicated for *anything*—especially for being gay.

Furthermore, I believe that spiritual abuse in all its insidious forms fuels addiction—as my play very personally illustrates. What do you fill your soul with when God no longer seems to be an option? Where do you turn when you no longer belong to your indigenous community? At the end of the day, then, *Confessions of a Mormon Boy* is my contribution to helping end spiritual abuse in our churches, mosques, synagogues, and families.

This play is about many things. But for me, it is about how I first learned to stop being a victim of spiritual abuse—and how I started to reclaim my values and a spirituality that works for me. It's been said that religion is for people who are afraid to go to hell. Spirituality is for people who have been to hell and don't want to go back! Religion and spirituality can be two very mutually exclusive things. And yet, I have to concede that religion *can* be a spiritual path for many, many people—though it seems to be the exception. Basic spiritual tools belong to everyone. Unfortunately, many religions put their own stamp on spiritual technology (i.e., prayer and meditation, reading inspired literature, gathering in fellowship, service, etc.), claiming theirs is the only way.

It has been rewarding to see men and women who have long abandoned their religion (often out of necessity or survival) leave the show with the possibility of reconciliation with their faith and a renewed commitment to spirituality in their lives—whatever that now needs to look like for them. It has also been humbling to meet other recovering sex workers after the show and hear their stories—and realize just how many of us have taken our spiritual gifts to the streets. (Commercial sex work includes prostitution, escorting, pimping, madaming, pornography, stripping, phone sex, adult cam work, erotic massage, or any other arena where you exchange sex or a sexual activity for money, services, or goods—whether a legal activity or not.) If churches could only get the impact of the loss of talent (and tithing!) they are missing out on by not embracing their LGBT members! (And the part this plays in fueling the rebelliousness of some of us!) I'm not a sociologist, but I'm alarmed as I see how many sex workers with magnificent spirits grew up with a religious upbringing that one day let them down. I don't know, there seems to be a connection . . . and some of us never make it back.

I would like to further propose that until we get "complete" with our parents, we cannot get complete with God. I think this is particularly true for those of us who grew up in a tribal-clan mentality with an unstated motto like: "If you're not Mormon, you're not family." Or "If you're not *straight*, you're not family." How I started to get over my anger and issues with my religious dad, in particular, is one of the most important dramatic arcs of the story and brings about the climax of the play. Making peace with my parents (and the spiritual abuse from *home*) has allowed me to start making peace with God. And it has been quite a homecoming! As it says in the Bible, may "the hearts of the fathers turn to the children, and the hearts of the children turn to their fathers."

No matter who we are, we all have a good victim story and can be held prisoner by that story. When we are in victim-mode, there is only one possibility—that of being a victim. And choosing victimization is not very sexy. When we become willing to give that up, we have all kinds of choices, our possibilities are endless, and miracles can occur. We are no longer our circumstances or our past. Who we are is literally Possibility itself: the possibility of being able to love and be loved by God and others.

I call my work "transformational theatre." My play is a true story of transformation (with elements of recovery) told by the person who lived it. It's reality theatre and is unabashedly purpose driven. I guess you can take the kid out of the cult, but you can't take the cult out of the kid! I hope my altruism isn't a turnoff. It's a by-product of my zealous upbringing. I further realize that yesterday's transformation is today's ego trip and tomorrow's relapse. So wish me luck!

Another purpose in writing was to illuminate the dilemma of those struggling to reconcile their dreams of becoming straight with the realities of being gay, and what it costs to accept or deny that truth—especially when children are involved. Some of us good fundamentalists got married to do the right thing. Many of us loved our straight spouses (as best we could) and were lucky enough to have children. And suddenly, the option of coming out became more and more acceptable. Sadly, many of us have had to choose between our authentic selves and waking up with our dear "spouse-friend" and beloved children each morning.

After my excommunication and divorce, I was concerned that if I were to die, there wouldn't be anyone I could fully trust to tell my young kids who I was, what happened, and how much their daddy loved them. So this play was originally written for my children. It seemed a matter of life and death that my kids (who are growing up in Utah, where it's debilitatingly shameful on the playground to have a gay dad) hear the complexities of this story in my own words—warts and all. It was my responsibility to tell it. As we are taught to do as Mormons, I have written a non-traditional family history. I felt it was my duty as a father and artist to do all I could to leave an accurate record behind to help them make sense of this nearly impossible situation.

This is serious personal family business going on before you. History is again repeating itself. As I mention in my play, my former father-in-law, Gerald Pearson, was a gay Mormon. I never got to meet him as he died of AIDS long before I married his oldest daughter, Emily. But I feel a kindred bond with him. My children are his grandchildren. Unfortunately, he never left a record for his children. But his ex-wife, Carol Lynn Pearson, told some of his story in her poignant autobiography *Good-bye, I Love You.*

If Gerald had lived, I believe he would have realized the vision Carol Lynn had for him. Even as she cared for him as he lay dying in her home she believed he "would be a light to point better directions to the gay community. And he would be the bridge he had so wanted to be to develop understanding of homosexuals to the larger world. He would take what he had been learning about what love really is and synthesize it into a wonderful message. He would write the things he only had reams of notes on. He would speak and people would listen. Surely that's what would happen. Surely Gerald would not die with his dreams unfulfilled."[†]

Gerald did not die in vain. For me, *Good-bye, I Love You* has been a template, a validating affirmation, a warning, a self-fulfilling prophecy, a guide, and, at the same time, a second chance. I have come to see this bizarre trans-generational synchronicity as a wonderful, painful, humbling, even joyful experience—rich in its potential for deeper understanding, healing, and forgiveness—and lots and lots of humor. As *Confessions of a Mormon Boy* has developed across the country, the story has hopefully become less and less about my connection to the extraordinary Pearson family, and more and more about my own spiritual journey.

The subject of homosexuality is controversial in and of itself—especially in Mormondom. When you are telling a personal story, when both

[†] *Carol Lynn Pearson,* Good-bye, I Love You *(New York: Random House, 1986)*

the general public and your children will read it or see it, homosexuality becomes an even more controversial subject. Some might say what Carol Lynn and I have done is not only shocking but greedy and possibly hurtful, that we've sold our "signs and tokens for money." We have broken taboos. But what we are both guilty of most, if anything, is following our hearts in attempting to make something poetic and positive out of our pain, starting with uncompromising honesty. "We are only as sick as our secrets." And if two generations can't testify to the transformative power of the truth gleaned from real life experience, then I'm giving up and getting re-baptized in the Mormon Church! (Would they take me back *now*?)

My ex-wife, Emily, is now writing her confessional. It's payback time—and I deserve it! But if you think Emily and I have a good story—wait 'til our kids write their book! (If they choose to finish this trilogy.)

∽

After finalizing the script for the Off-Broadway run of *Confessions of a Mormon Boy* (a process best termed as "distilling"), I found I had stacks of material left over. Here then, are many of the things I wanted to say on stage, but couldn't for one reason or another—not the least of which was time. Ninety minutes of me talking about myself without an intermission was the maximum audience bladders—and my director—would allow. I've expanded my "comic/dramatic autobiographical monologue mingled with scripture and song" for this book. Everything you read here has been performed in one version or another (in a reading or production) as the play developed on its way to a commercial Off-Broadway run.

I've also included an excerpt from the original Utah version of the play. This more whimsical script served as the world premiere of the play in Salt Lake City. As you will see, it is drastically different in form and tone—but it will always be my favorite. It is my original "funny valentine to Mormonism." There is also an epilogue, an afterword describing how the play developed, and other features and resources that give more context to the project and my gay Mormon world, including my excommunication letter and production photos.

Everything in *Confessions of a Mormon Boy*, to the best of my knowledge and recollection—is 99 percent true, with the rest being 100 percent emotionally and poetically honest. I've admittedly taken some creative license by recreating a few scenes, embellishing some dialogue for comedic purposes, altering some chronology for dramatic purposes, and compressing a few characters into one. Artistic license has been taken in portraying certain characters and preserving the anonymity of others—but all characters are actual people from my life, events that actually happened, and institutions which I was a part of. As we say in Mormondom when we bear our testimonies: "I know, with every fiber of my being—that this play is true!"

The one-person show genre does not allow for my entire story to be told. There are so many things to share and expound upon. They will have to wait to be expressed in other ways and at a future time. I hope that I have made the strongest points and that the blanks will be filled in with thoughtfulness, compassion, intelligence, and sensitivity by the reader. As it says in *The Book of Mormon*, "And now, if there are faults they are the mistakes of men; wherefore, condemn not . . . " In other words, "I cannot write the hundredth part."

I have found sanctuary in the theatre—the temple of humanism. In a way, the theatre is where I go to commune and worship—often eight shows a week. It's where, in the words of one of Shakespeare's greatest human beings, King Lear, "None doth offend." I hope you enjoy my "Orpheus Descends" love story and my post-post Modern prodigal tale about the humanization of a Mormon boy. I don't think St. Augustine would approve of some of my confessions, but then again, I'm not Catholic.

The Brethren of the Church said I could appeal my excommunication if I wanted to. Instead, I am taking my appeal to the stage and am offering this play as my prayer. And since my Higher Power has a sense of humor—and a touch of sarcasm, too—maybe, just maybe, if we laugh (and cry) enough together, we can laugh me right into heaven. Then the Devil will really have something to chuckle about!

Blessings, and keep smiling!

Steven Fales,
"Transformin' Mormon"
Salt Lake City, Utah, September 2006

PART ONE

The Production

(Photo: Miele Klein)

The Smile

The Mormon smile is made by first thinking how deeply grateful and blessed you are to belong to "the only true and living church upon the face of the whole earth." As one of the Chosen, this thought brings you incomparable glee that just can't be contained. Your smile's size is proportionate to just how many Mormon pioneer ancestors you had sweat and freeze across the Plains. If you are truly Mormon royalty, your smile will be enormous! Imagine your favorite hymn or Disney's "It's a Small World" playing over and over in your head as you compulsively smile your charming, wholesome, flashy, adorably irresistible, perky Osmond smile.

The smile comes through the eyes, not just the teeth—they twinkle and sparkle, eyebrows raised high. As you smile, your head is cocked a little to the right to show the world just how cute and sincere you are. There's maybe a little shrug and a giggle of delight—perhaps an unconscious condescending wink. There's a spring in your step. You want to have the best smile possible, so brush and floss your teeth after every meal. Teeth whitening is rarely necessary because, as a good member of the Church, you don't drink wine or coffee or use tobacco in the first place. The most precious and righteous Mormons do not need braces. Many find that their smiles help them read in the dark. They also find it hard to kiss, as puckering is difficult with overdeveloped smiling muscles.

Your smile can be used for many things, but its official purpose is to attract others to the Church (and other multilevel marketing campaigns—think Amway). You smile all the time because you never know how or when your smile might convert another to the source of true happiness—"mainstream" Mormonism. (Just one smile can metastasize the world!) If you're ever caught not smiling, you will be held responsible for all the souls who would have been saved had you been smiling as you should have been. Some of your salvation may be deducted in the next life if you're not careful. You must avoid this and any guilt with every fiber of your being. As it says in the Bible, "Let your light so shine." So smile brightly! Sing a hymn: *"Scatter sunshine all along your way..."* or *"Jesus wants me for a sunbeam to shine for him each day..."*.

Remember, in the end it's all about who wins—er—can be the nicest. And nice winners smile. Even when crying, continue smiling at all times—even when you are alone. (Someone may be watching!) And if you ever feel like swearing, smile instead. (Kill 'em with kindness!)

But don't think because Mormons smile *ad nauseum* they don't know what pain and suffering is. They do. It's just that they have a hope and uncompromising optimism that comes from their faith—and their proud pioneer legacy. They can endure all things, including any tragedy, because one day they will live eternally with their "elect" loved ones again in paradise. They live *into* a glorious future (they believe that they will one-day become gods themselves) that transforms their present, making them extraordinary neighbors. (And they live an average of ten years longer than you will—having the last laugh. They will be re-writing herstory.) Their burdens are lighter than others because they alone lay claim to the gift of the Holy Ghost—sent to comfort them in their times of need. But only if they are worthy of such blessings. And, as luck would have it, they usually are. Well, most of them are—the *straight* ones.

Play History

Confessions of a Mormon Boy was originally produced Off-Broadway by Mormon Boy Productions, LLC in association with Brian Malk, James Fales, Kyle Kimoto, and Carleton and Sharon Spaulding at the SoHo Playhouse in New York City. Opening night was February 5, 2006 (Super Bowl Sunday), with previews beginning January 27, 2006. The play closed April 16, 2006 (Easter Sunday), having played 80 performances with 12 preview performances.

The play was nominated for a New York Outer Critics Circle Award for Outstanding Solo Performance. (Sir Antony Sher winning for *Primo* which played on Broadway that season.) The play had previously been a breakout hit of the 2004 New York International Fringe Festival, where it received an Overall Excellence Award for Solo Show.

Confessions was written, created, and performed by Steven Fales; the director was Jack Hofsiss. The assistant director was Ken Daigle; the set and lighting design was by Tim Saternow; the costume design was by Ellis Tillman; the sound design was by Robert Kaplowitz; additional music arrangements were by Clive Romney; hair was by Alfieri Salon, New York; the assistant set designer was Brett McCormack; the assistant lighting designer was Joe Chapman; the acting coach was Holly Villaire; the voice and dialect coach was David Alan Stern; the production stage managers were Charles M. Turner III and BJ Forman. The publicist was Sam Rudy and Dale Heller of Sam Rudy Media Relations; Graphic Design/Advertising was by Chris Major and Regis Albrecht of CHMajor Group; Web Site Marketing by Michael Spaulding, Markus Hartel, and Jim Glaub; Production Management was by Ben Heller of Aurora Productions; Production Carpenter was Derek Dickenson; Production Electrician was Tom Dyer; Production sound was David A. Arnold; Light Board operators were Sarah Nogaim and Jim Sparnon; Rehearsal Studios were Theatre Row Studios and Shepler Studios; Group Sales by Janette Roush of Broadway.com; Marketing consultant Joseph Craig of Nielsen Entertainment; Wardrobe was by Betsy C. Liegel; Marketing was by Hugh Hysell and Jessica Hinds of HHC Marketing; Assistant to the Producer was Heather Hill; Production Photos were by Carol Rosegg; Publicity Photos and Cover Photography by Dorothy Shi; Theatre owners and executive directors were Darren Lee Cole and Faith Mulvihill; Box Office General Manager was Gabriel Voytas; Legal Counsel was Jason Baruch of Franklin, Wenrib, Rudell & Vassallo, P.C.; Payroll was Martha Palubniak of Axium International; Insurance: Anthony Pittari of DeWitt Stern Group, Inc.; Accountant was Robert Fried of Fried & Kowgios Partners, LLP; General Management was by Seth M. Goldstein, Elisabeth Bayer, Anne Love and Anthony Merced of The Splinter Group.

The budget for the commercial New York run was $315,000. Most of the money came from straight investors from Salt Lake City, San Diego, and Las Vegas, with other investors from Connecticut, Florida, Illinois, Oregon, and New York.

The recordings of the little boy speaking and singing in the play were originally recordings of Steven Fales singing as a young child.

The play was previously presented at the Coconut Grove Playhouse, Arnold Mittelman, Producing Artistic Director and by The New York International Fringe Festival, a production of The Present Company.

Other significant milestones in the development of the play toward its Off-Broadway run:

Caroline's on Broadway, five-minute standup comedy routine (for the American Comedy Institute), June 2001 (also at Standup New York and Don't Tell Mama)
NYC apartment readings, Summer and Fall 2001
Sunstone Symposium reading, Salt Lake City, August 2001
Reading at Spaulding's Home, Salt Lake City, October 2001
Salt Lake City, world premiere (original Utah version), Rose Wagner Performing Arts Center, November 2001, (extended by popular demand).
Gamofite (Gay Mormon Fathers) Retreat reading, Maryland/ Washington D.C., April 2002

NYC workshop (gentile version), Jose Quintero Theatre on
   Forty-second Street, June 2002
San Francisco run (New Conservatory Theatre), August 2002;
   (extended by popular demand)
San Francisco reading at NCT (escorting/drugs added), August 2002
Las Vegas run, Clark County Library Theatre (National Affirmation
   Conference), September 2002; (author's father attended for the
   first time)
Salt Lake City II (escorting/drugs first performed), Rose Wagner
   Performing Arts Center, September 2002
Writing Workshop with Jack Hofsiss in New York, October 2002
National Gamofite Conference Reading, San Diego, January 2003
Miami run (Coconut Grove Playhouse), March 2003
Basic Rights Oregon Benefit Staged Reading, November 2003
Desert AIDS Project Benefit Staged Reading, Palm Springs,
   November 2003
Portland (OR) Run (Hollywood Theatre), May 2004
New York International Fringe Festival, August 2004, break-out Hit,
   extra performance added.
Salt Lake City III (GLBT Center of Utah Benefit), September 2004
Connecticut Repertory Theatre/UConn, December 2004
Chicago Run (Bailiwick Repertory Theatre), January 2005
   (Extended by popular demand.)
San Francisco II (New Conservatory Theatre), April 2005
San Diego Run (Diversionary Theatre), July 2005, Extended run
   breaking all box office records in twenty-year history
Lincoln Center Theatre, New York City, The Point Foundation
   Benefit, December 5, 2005. Mitzi Newhouse Theatre, (sold-out,
   star-studded event).
San Diego II (Diversionary Theatre), December 2005
Off-Broadway Run, SoHo Playhouse, Opening Night,
   February 5, 2006
National/International tour planned: Atlanta, Austin, Los Angeles,
   Boston, London

"More than anything, I wanted to be happy."
(Carol Rosegg)

"How I loved just holding my children."
(Carol Rosegg)

The Complete Monologue Script
of *Confessions of a Mormon Boy*

(COMPILED FROM ALL PAST DRAFTS,
INCLUDING THE FINAL OFF-BROADWAY SCRIPT)

PRE-SHOW MUSIC: "BATTLE HYMN OF THE REPUBLIC" AND OTHER SONGS BY GRAMMY AWARD–WINNING MORMON TABERNACLE ("MO-TAB") CHOIR

VOICEOVER GREETING: (*"When the Saints Go Marching In" plays underneath*): "Brothers and Sisters: Welcome to the SoHo Playhouse. We'd like to take this opportunity to remind you to turn off all electronic noise-making devices. And, in accordance with Actors' Equity Association, there is no recording or photography of any kind allowed during the performance. Also, no smoking, drinking, swearing, fornicating, light-mindedness, loud laughter, evil-speaking of the Lord's anointed, or any other unholy and impure practice—except by the actor. The playwright/performer accepts all liability and responsibility for any references to The Church of Jesus Christ of Latter-day Saints in his play. The SoHo Playhouse, its affiliates, family members and domestic partners, do not necessarily share the views of the playwright, and are to be held blameless on Judgment Day, and in any court in the state of Utah. Thank you. 'Preciate ya! And enjoy the show!"

(*In the dark we hear a scratchy, amateur recording of a perky young child speaking and singing. During the recording the lights come up on a thirty-something male actor dressed in a BYU T-shirt. There is a bench center stage and a small table with a water bottle and a copy of* The Book of Mormon *and other papers stage left.*

There is a coat stand with various costume pieces stage right. Throughout the play the storyteller takes on the persona and voice of each of the different characters of which he speaks. The Off-Broadway production ran approximately 90 minutes without intermission.)

Okay, everybody ready?
It will begin now!

(Scatting.)

Okay.
If you are singing about flowers,
You are singing about joy.
You are the only one
That changes the world.

(Scatting.)   This is me. I think I was about
                                         five years old.

If you are playing
You pick flowers   That's my little brother
For your mom or dad   singing backup.
Or baby sister.

(Scatting.)   I just made up songs like this.
                                         Mormons record everything.

If you are singing
Sing about flowers.   This is the chorus.
If you are singing,
Sing about joy.   I really sell it here!
If you are singing,
Sing about the whole world.   *(Snaps fingers and sings along.)*
So be sure to sing about the flowers.

                                         Now with a song like that,
                                         could there be any question in
                                         anyone's mind that I was gay?

Welcome, Brothers and Sisters. I'm Steven Fales and I'm a Mormon. And that's why I smile like this. (*Smiles*.) So I'm a gay Mormon. Which I think makes me an oxy-Mormon .... My last name, Fales—not F-A-I-L-S, F-A-L-E-S—is an old Welsh name meaning "son of Fagel," spelled F-A-G-e-l. Fagel, also pronounced *faygeleh* means, "to be glad," which is a synonym for "happy" or "gay"—and that's also why I smile like this! (*Smiles*.) I was recently excommunicated from my church for the "practice of homosexuality." Apparently the Brethren didn't like some of the folks I was smilin' at ...

VOICEOVER: (*with an interrogating spotlight*) "Brothers and Sisters: So-called gays, or *gender-disorienteds*, may have certain inclinations which are powerful and which may be difficult to control. But if they violate moral law, they are subject to discipline. The death penalty was exacted in the days of Israel for such wrong-doing. Remember, God made no man a pervert. For those who have strayed, we promise homosexuality can be cured. You can totally recover from its tentacles and free yourself of your master, the devil—Satan. Don't be selfish, lazy and weak. How can you know you cannot change until your knees are sore from praying and your knuckles bloody from knocking on the Lord's door for help?"

Would you like to see the scars on my knuckles? If they only knew how hard I tried to prevent this. Believe it or not, I never asked to be gay.

I'm sixth generation. That makes me a DNA Mormon. My people settled Utah. I'm the oldest of six kids and the oldest grandchild on both sides. And thanks to a little polygamy here and there, I have a huge extended family—hundreds of Mormons. We all smile like this. (*Smiles*)

Except my Greek great-grandfather. I don't think he understood what all the smiling was about. He eventually went back to Greece, but he stuck around just long enough to mix his great, big, passionate Greek Orthodox DNA with Anglo-Saxon propriety. That's why my boyfriends smile the way they do ...

My favorite scripture growing up was in *The Book of Mormon*: (*Reads*)

"Men are that they might have joy. Consider the blessed and happy state of those that keep the commandments of God. For behold, they are blessed in all things, both temporal and spiritual; and if they hold out faithful to the end they are received into heaven that thereby they may dwell with God in a state of never-ending happiness."

More than anything, I wanted to be happy. And though I was on the fast track to exaltation and eternal bless, something started to happen. One day I noticed I wasn't smiling anymore. Even when I was smiling, I wasn't *really* smiling. And though you really couldn't see it on the outside—I could feel it on the inside. And I wondered if, in this life, I would ever really smile again . . .

∽

My parents' Mormon marriage was practically arranged. When my mother found out she was pregnant, two weeks after the honeymoon, at eighteen, she threw herself on her bed in their dark basement apartment in Provo, Utah, and in her desperation, loneliness, and morning sickness cried out, "Please, God, just send me a friend." She says when I was born it was as if a ray of sunshine burst through the clouds. And so I came to Earth, trailing clouds of glory (and fairy dust) unto a mundane, macho Mormon world.

I was one of those obnoxious perfect children that rarely ever cried. Mom says she kept having more children so she could have another me. (Don't tell my brothers and sisters that!) She also says as I was growing up, each year she was amazed that I was still alive. She says I was too good for this earth. So from a very early age I was cursed with feeling I was somehow undeservedly and singularly *special*.

One of my favorite things to do as a kid was watch our favorite Mormon mascots on *The Donny & Marie Show* with my family every Sunday night. While most boys my age wanted to be Donny and marry Marie, I wanted to marry Donny and *be* Marie. I was teased incessantly by other boys at school for acting like a girl, so my father really poured on the steam when I was about eight years old. He put me in Little League and taught me how to hit and run like a man.

He also taught me about sex. He took me out to the cows and told me how that one Black Angus was going to put his penis in the other and that one day I'd do that to my wife and it would feel really good and warm.

I was involved in my church-sponsored Boy Scout troop. I became an Eagle Scout (the highest rank in scouting). "A scout is trustworthy, loyal, helpful, friendly, courteous, kind, obedient, cheerful, thrifty, brave, clean, and reverent." I promised "to keep myself physically strong, mentally awake, and morally straight." I could tie knots, canoe, wrestle, ride horses, and shoot guns with the best of them, but secretly my favorite merit badges were cooking and textiles.

And for anyone who's still not convinced, I'm famous for the Liberace impersonation I did at a church talent show when I was seventeen. I came out from the wings holding a candelabra, wearing my high school madrigal prince charming costume (I designed it myself, sewed on all the pearls by hand). I had on tights and my mom's full-length chinchilla. I played "Rustles of Spring", then swapped "funeral potato" recipes with the Relief Society sisters on the front row. "Not too much sour cream, Sister Edwards!"

Now it might be fun to continue to frolic in my past like many "gay plays," and reminisce about how effeminate I was (and defective I felt) growing up. All those boring over-achieving stories and miserable, character-rebuilding, campy, cliché, stereotypical, gloriously delicious gay anecdotes from elementary school through high school, but let's just cut to the chase and get to the point of this Ethel Mormon monologue.

༺

Now when a Mormon boy turns nineteen, he is expected to serve a formal, full-time, volunteer, two-year mission for the Church.

My dad and all my uncles went, but I was *not* gonna go. I was an exception. I was gonna convert millions through my singularly unique musical testimony. But one day—I was in the shower—and I heard this voice that surprised me:

VOICEOVER: "Steven, you could go on a mission and really make a difference, *and* you might actually like it."

"But I want to be the next Osmond! Donny! Or *Marie . . . ?*"

Deep down I believed that "Christ takes the slums out of people and people take themselves out of the slums." So I filled out the paperwork, was determined worthy, and was called by the prophet to serve the Lord in Portugal. I was off to the Missionary Training Center where I would spend the next two months twenty-four seven with twenty-five hundred beautiful homophobic young men while learning the missionary discussions in Portuguese. It was hard work. And sometimes I'd get depressed and wonder if all those good Catholics were really gonna go to hell if *I* didn't get through to them . . . But I loved Portugal—and being enlisted in God's army. I was a leader and was known as the elder who played the piano and could sing:

(*Sings chorus from "How Great Thou Art," in Portuguese*)

> *Canta minha alma*
> *Então a ti, Senhor.*
> *Grandioso es tu,*
> *Grandioso es tu.*

I baptized a lot of people. And it was inspiring to see how the Restored Gospel seemed to transform so many lives. There was a young single woman we taught who had been thinking of killing herself—she was so depressed she wanted to die. After she was baptized she was a new person. She was so happy! She said that she could feel the Holy Spirit working in her life. Then there was this refugee family from Angola. The father gave up drinking to be baptized. And for the first time, he became the father his family had always needed him to be. I even helped convert an entire family who had once been Jehovah's Witnesses. Families were on their way to becoming *Forever Families.*

But I feel my greatest accomplishment came in helping one particular young elder. He was gender-disoriented. He was gayer than I was! And he wasn't at all happy. And one night we talked about it. Just talked! We didn't kiss or fall in love or have sex. And later at mission conferences we'd give each other a big hug, look each other in the eye, and just . . . *know.*

And at the end of my mission during the final interview with the mission president, I offered the closing prayer in Portuguese. All I could say through my tears was, *"Nosso Pai Celestial, sou grato por minha missão."*

"Heavenly Father, thank you for my mission."

℘

After I got back to the States, like all really good Mormon boys (and like my dad), I went to BYU—Brigham Young University. (Where tuition is discounted for members.) It's in Provo, Utah, where I was born. ("Go, Cougars! *Woof! Woof! Woof! Woof! Woof!*") I got a partial voice scholarship, and I paid the bills as a model for the BYU art department. (Don't get excited, they make you wear a Speedo!)

The *real* reason for going to the "Y" was to find a good Mormon wife. My salvation depended on it. You have to be married to a woman to get into heaven! So as I waited to find my eternal female companion, I knew I was going far in the musical theatre department when I made the Young Ambassadors. (*Smiles.*)

Now, the Young Ambassadors was an elite group of performing missionaries that the Church used to charm nations that had not yet been receptive to letting the missionaries prostitute. I mean *proselytize!* (A preliminary warm-up to hosting the 2002 Winter "Molympic" Games where the Church would produce a free admission spectacular designed to convert the world.) They poured tons of money into our shows, which were a kaleidoscope of music, dance, colorful lights and costumes, and above all—smiles! It was a cross between *Lawrence Welk, The Donny & Marie Show,* Disney, and the worst of Andrew Lloyd Webber. "*Meow!*"

Not only did you have to be beautiful and talented to be a "Y.A.", you had to adhere to the highest moral standards as set forth in the Honor Code; namely, no sex, drugs, alcohol, tobacco, caffeine, R-rated movies, tattoos, piercings, facial hair, or shorts above the knee.

So, naturally, it was on tour with Young Ambassadors that I had my first (*Whispered*) homosexual experience. This guy was so straight-acting you never would have known. And such a good kisser! I was floored when *he* turned our friendship sexual. ("Homosexuality does not exist at the Lord's University!") The few times we got together were incredible. It wasn't just erotic. It was intimate and expansive.

I remember this one morning, in Salina, Kansas, walking from our motel room to the tour bus with the biggest smile on my face. (I finally understood what all the love songs were about.) And I remember thinking, "How can I be feeling what I recognize as the Spirit so strongly when I've just done something so abominable?"

Looking back, what we actually did seems pretty naïve and innocent. Nevertheless and notwithstanding, I was in a bind. An irreconcilable incongruity existed between what I felt was natural and right, and what the Church taught was Heavenly Father's Plan for me. The closer we got to Provo, the more the guilt set in. So like the good Mormon boy I was, I turned myself in.

(*Speaks on the phone*) "Hi, Bishop. It's Brother Fales. *Fales*. No, 'F' as in 'fabulous . . . ' I don't think I can keep my church calling. Well, I'm not worthy. I had sexual relations on tour . . . with a guy."

He told me he would gladly pay for my therapy, and to "stay away from that predator!"

So, I started seeing an LDS woman (a Latter-day Saint) who was a clinical hypnotherapist:

"Hmmm. We're gonna have to work on your S.S.A."

"My what?"

"*Same-Sex Attraction*! You see, you have a compulsive sexual addiction. Do you look at pornography?"

"No! But I get turned on watching BYU football games . . . "

"S.S.A! What about self-abuse?"

"Masturbation?"

"*Shhhh*! Uh-huh . . . ?"

"Once in a while. I didn't even touch myself the first eighteen months of my mission."

"Self-abuse causes homosexuality!"

"Then wouldn't everyone be gay?"

"No! Now, have you ever been sexually abused by anyone other than yourself?"

"No."

"I knew it! Denial! Suppressed memories! Be brave. You can face this. Take some deep breaths. We are gonna find out who violated you as a child!"

So we probed my early childhood. We went down every path of memory we could. But we still couldn't uncover who made me gay.

"There is still a way! Give me permission to 'muscle test' you."

Now by rubbing her finger and thumb together, she could determine—by the change in texture of her skin—the answer to *anything*. She discovered that I had been aborted "one, two, three, four, five, six, seven—*seven* times before making it to Earth. That's very traumatic for a fetus! Now Brother Fales, I'm so sorry, but I need to inform ya that based on my advanced kinesthetic technique (which is never wrong!), your father sexually abused you before you were . . . *one!* And that's why sometimes you feel just a little bit queer."

I wanted a second opinion.

So I went to LDS Social Services to find a real psychologist. He told me all about Pavlov's dog. "The dog would salivate just hearing a bell. Homosexuality's the same way. Just change the stimulus and you'll stop salivating. Heck, I used to get a hard-on every time I saw a motorcycle."

I decided not to go back. I wasn't into leather . . . yet.

Then I was given a book that had just come out: *Reparative Therapy of Male Homosexuality.* It said that homosexuality was preventable and treatable—without all that electro-shock therapy. It gave me hope. My parents encouraged me. I got blessing from my dad. I was gonna be okay.

So after I felt God had forgiven me, I threw myself into school and dating girls. But the girls I dated wanted to marry the butch M.B.A. majors with the new SUVs. I didn't even have a B-I-K-E. After one particularly devastating break up, I said, "Lord, if I'm gonna be single, just help me be chaste and send me good friends . . . "

A year later I met Emily Pearson.

∽

Emily and I could talk for hours on end about anything. And what a catch! She was tall, blonde, blue-eyed, gorgeous, funny, spiritual, charismatic, cosmopolitan *and* domestic, talented—she'd played

Anita in *West Side Story* at BYU! Everything and more you could ask for in a Mormon wife—and the mother of your children. And because her mother, Carol Lynn Pearson, was a famous Mormon writer, she's what we call "*Mormon Royalty*".

Carol Lynn Pearson. Her most famous work was her autobiography, *Good-bye, I Love You*. It told the story of her relationship with her gay husband, Gerald. After four children they divorced but remained close friends. He was part of that first wave of men in San Francisco that contracted AIDS. Well, she brought him home to die. And this was in the early eighties when no one was talking about AIDS, let alone from a compassionate *Mormon* perspective. The book was originally published by Random House, and it put her on all the talk shows from *Oprah* to *Geraldo*. They were featured in *People* magazine. Their wedding picture even replaced Batboy on the cover of *Weekly World News*, "Wife Brings Gay Hubby Home to Die of AIDS!" Her book made her the patron saint of gay Mormon men and women.

So as Emily and I got more serious in our dating, I thought I'd read up on Em's family. I started reading her mother's book at eleven o'clock at night and finished it at four in the morning. I couldn't put it down—or stop crying. From the very first sentence, it was as if you could replace the name Gerald with *Steven*. I knew nothing about the gay lifestyle. And what I read terrified and at the same time called to me.

When Emily's dad came out of the closet, they moved from Utah to California. Carol Lynn and the kids lived in Walnut Creek; Gerald moved to the Castro. When he'd visit the kids on the weekend, Carol Lynn would drop him off at BART.

(*Reads from* Good-bye, I Love You.)

"Good night, Private Pearson," [she] called after.
"Hmmmm?"
"You look like you're in the Army. Take care of yourself."

Again [she] watched the lights of the train disappear into the distance. The Army, [she] thought. He did look like he was in the Army. And what a strange army. Thousands of men who have rejected the traditional male institutions have built a counterculture army of their own. Where is the sergeant who is calling out all these orders? Who says you have to cut your hair so you look like a skinned rabbit? Who says you have to wear the standard uniform, the plaid shirt and the tight Levi's? Who says you have to put more money than you can manage into keeping the body beautiful? Who says you have to subscribe to the newspapers in which men advertise their sexual specialties? Where is the sergeant who demands that you march to a certain rhythm and chant certain words? "I am a man!" they shout at Fort Ord, marching and waving their bayonets. "I am a man!" they shout in San Francisco, marching and waving their banners. Where there are armies there is usually destruction. And the women stay home as women always have and watch and wait to pick up the pieces. [She] watched Gerald fall into step and [she] cursed the unseen sergeant of Castro Street.

The Church was telling me I was straight. But this book, and my heart, was telling me I was *gay*.

I didn't want to be gay. I didn't want to be *Gerald*. I didn't want to be unhappy and get AIDS. I wanted a family! And yet what was I *thinking* dating a girl? And of all girls, *this* girl who had suffered so much already. She adored her father. It broke her heart when he died. She was only sixteen. The title of the book came from her. "Good-bye, I love you" were the last words she said to her dad. What kind of a joke were the gods playing on us? For what it was worth, Emily and I were falling in love! But maybe Emily was the one who could save me from this fate ...

I had to tell her what I had done in Young Ambassadors. It was all over and repented of, but I *had* to tell her. When I said we needed to talk, she said, "Well, I know where!" And she took me to the park across the street from where she grew up as a little girl. Across from the same house where her mother found out her husband had been cheating on her with other men.

I told her. *Everything*. But I was sure it would never happen again. And I left it in her hands and let her decide if she still wanted to continue to date. After a week of tears, to my relief, *she did*! So we went to pre-marriage counseling and talked it through. Our church leaders assured us and gave us the okay. "You're doing what's right, brother and sister. We *promise*, the Lord'll take care of the rest!"

So just before we got engaged we flew to California to meet *her mother*. There I was sitting on the beach with *the* Mormon matriarch with her signature short white hair and sparkling blue eyes. I told her I was really moved by her book.

"Well, Steven. If there's anything we need to talk about on that subject, *now would be a good time to do it . . . ?*"

(*Laughing*) "Oh, no! Not me! I would never do that to Emily and you!"

Emily was sitting next to me and watched on as I brushed her mom's question aside. We had decided together, before we got there, *not* to tell her mother. We were gonna write a different story.

We had faith in this new "reparative therapy", in the Church, and in ourselves. We could lick it! We were supposed to be together. We had fasted and prayed. We had all the right confirmations. We would succeed where the previous generation had failed. We would defy *Good-bye, I Love You* and write *Hello, I Love You.*

I wanted to propose in a way that physicalized our commitment and would symbolize the ups and downs of the journey ahead. I proposed on the top of Mt. Timpanogos—the tallest mountain around. When we finally made it down the mountain it was pitch black, we were soaking wet, and the ranger had towed my car.

After a long Mormon engagement (four whole months), we were married. Sealed for "time and all eternity" by the same general authority who married her parents in the same, exact temple. I sang at our reception:

(*Sings theme from* Love Story)

> *How long does it last?*
> *Can love be measured by the hours in a day?*
> *I have no answers now, but this much I can say—*
> *I know I'll need her till the stars all burn away,*
> *And she'll be there.*

We were both virgins on our wedding night. The shining example of what a newlywed couple could be. The Tom & Nicole of Mormondom. Except for one thing. Unlike Tom, I was taller than she was . . .

∽

After graduating from BYU, we moved to Las Vegas—where I actually grew up. (That's another reason I'm an oxy-Mormon. And another reason I smile like this, "Hey!" You can't do anything Sin City is famous for. You can't drink or gamble in the casinos. But you can sure as heck own 'em!) I was performing at an amusement park on the family-friendly strip and was working at the University of Nevada, Las Vegas. (Go Rebels, *"Woof! Woof! Woof! Woof! Woof!*) One morning I was taking some books across campus to the library and the Bi, Gay, Lesbian, Transgender Student Association had put all these banners up: "National Coming Out Day! Show your pride by wearing purple!"

I was disgusted. I was like, "How *dare* they infect this campus with their politics!" And I'm walking along, looking down at the sidewalk and there were all these purple flyers taped to the concrete. And I'm like, "Ugh!" And I looked down and, *"Aagh!* I'm wearing a purple turtleneck!" I looked around. Had anyone seen me? I raced home and changed my shirt. But I couldn't change my colors.

Later that night I was at my dad's house and we were alone in the back.

"Dad, I don't think I can *do* this. I think I am *gay.*"

"Son, you *can* do this. You are *not* gay."

Emily and I became pregnant! We got the ultrasound and we were having a boy. I thought, "Oh! How can *I* be a father to a *boy*? I don't know how to do this!" I wasn't able to be like, (*Sings from "Soliloquy" from* Carousel) *"My boy, Bill, I will see that he's named after me!"* But I just committed to loving him. I was so excited to protect and provide for my new little family. I could play this role!

I watched my son being born with such tenderness and awe. I blessed him in front of the congregation just like my father had blessed me. He was my Simba and I was Mufasa taking my rightful place in the patriarchal "Circle of Life." And every night when I'd come home from work, I would pick up my sleeping son from his crib and hold him. Emily and I would sing together:

(*Sings from "Angel Lullaby" from Carol Lynn Pearson's musical* My Turn On Earth)

So, sleep, sleep 'til the darkness ends,
Guarded by your angel friends.

How I loved just holding my son. And dancing with him to ABBA songs in the living room of whatever cramped apartment we were in at the time (*Singing*) *"Angel eyes, one look and you're hypnotized ..."* And we'd fly and fly and fly ...

∽

I took my provider role seriously, even though my father warned me that getting a Master of Fine Arts in acting was getting a degree in "recess" and I'd never be a good provider. "You should be a doctor like me! Do you think you can just get by on your smile?"

I had to be selective about which graduate school to attend. They'd have to be tolerant of my being Mormon and *straight*. Emily had the talent, I was getting the degree—just in case the Lord ever needed me to teach acting at BYU.

The University of Connecticut gave me a full ride. (Go Huskies! *Woof! Woof! Woof! Woof! Woof!*) And the religion practiced on campus was humanism. I didn't want to believe I was human. I hated humans. They were so ... *human*. I was a Mormon. And above all (dang it!), I was a *straight*, Mormon—Republican. (Reagan was Moses in my family!)

Like I said, I took my provider role seriously and took out student loans so my wife wouldn't have to work and could stay at home with our son—and all our future kids. I had to navigate treacherous secular waters. I was busy teaching, performing, and taking a full course load—in addition to magnifying all my church callings. All the classes seemed to blend into one long three-year course: *post-modern, existential, iconoclastic, deconstructionist funk.* (I kind of liked it!) But on top of it all, my S.S.A. got more intense. So I thought I'd conquer it by trying something I had never done before, *pornographia heterosexualis.* (I think it's Latin!)

I hadn't read or been exposed to any pornography growing up. Certainly not gay porn let alone the *appropriate* porn. (Unless you want to count Las Vegas billboards!) I thought about it for a while and finally got up the courage to prove I was straight. I went out at twenty-seven and bought my first *Playboy*. I took it home and secretly pulled it out one night when Emily and our son were away visiting her mother in California. There I was, masturbating with all my heart to this voluptuous blonde in the centerfold. It seemed to take forever. Until that blonde began to look a lot like . . . Donny Osmond.

Now my school wanted to do *Angels in America*. I begged them not to do it. I just winced when I read it. First of all, I was Republican. I was sure to be cast as the Mormon who ends up leaving his wife for another man. And my pregnant wife was sure to be there opening night! So, lucky for me, they decided to do a new adaptation of the musical *Hair* instead, where they took everything Vietnam out and put everything HIV in. And they thought, "Wouldn't it be clever if we took that wholesome Mormon boy and cast him as Woof, a Catholic gay activist? Let's have him sing 'Sodomy' and then 'White Boys.'"

So rather than wage another fight with the head of the department, I thought I'd show them what this wholesome Mormon boy could do. Like the good M.F.A. actor I was being trained to be, I decided to do a little character research on the *homoerotic*. I went down to the local video store (where we rented Barney the Dinosaur videos) and rented a male strip video. It was the closest I would go to gay porn.

One night, when Emily and our son were still in California, I pulled it out and stuck it in. As soon as I pressed play, I was pre-cumming all over the place. I was leaking out of control. A woman had never done that to me before. Never! And I could cum over and over and over again! What do you do with that? That's when I knew I was really in a bind. If you took a *Cosmo* magazine and a *Men's Muscle & Fitness* and put them in front of me, there was no question which magazine cover my body would point to.

So I did the show. I was ferocious! Straight guys told me I turned them on. The reviews simply said, "Fales' 'White Boys' is a howl!" Each night at the curtain call I felt this rush of electric authenticity. "Good Morning, Starshine!" It was so freeing. But it was so scary. I had way too much at stake to be feeling this free. So after the production, I slammed the door on exploring my sexuality any further. We were expecting. Nothing would stop us from multiplying and replenishing the earth with our second child, our daughter! Not even S.S.A.! And I had become the church choir director in nearby Providence, Rhode Island. (*Smiles*)

∽

Shortly after another graduation, with funds low and credit cards max'd out, it was either commute into New York for auditions or buy diapers. I bought the Pampers. But since it was a callback this time, I scraped the spare change together and drove two-and-a-half hours into the city. After the audition, I decided to go really off-budget and bought a half-priced ticket to a new Broadway play, *The Beauty Queen of Leenane*. So I got to the theatre, sat down and dived into the program. And this *guy* came and sat right next to me. He was so good-looking—so open and friendly. He had this great energy.

"Altoid?" he asked.

"Do I need one?"

"No."

"Sure."

We started talking. I didn't mention my wife and kids like I usually did. I wanted to see what would happen if I didn't hide. There was an instant connection. And it was so hard to focus on this dark Irish play when I was so lit up by this dirty blond.

At intermission, I decided to move up to some better seats that were vacant. I asked him if he wanted to, too. To my delight and horror, he said yes. We lingered for a bit after the show and then walked to Times Square. He asked if I wanted to go meet a "friend" that worked at the hotel. I just played naïve: "No. I've gotta drop these resumes off at my manager's on Christopher Street." So we wished each other well and shook hands with a little more intention than normal. And we went in opposite directions.

And when I got to the subway, I turned around and I could see him looking for me through the crowd:

✐

VOICEOVER: "Joseph in the Bible ran! He just left his garments in Poti-
phar's wife's hands and ran!"

So I did! To the end of the platform. And I turned my collar up and my
back to the crowd. I was so relieved when the subway finally came. I got off
at Christopher Street. Well, he came bounding up from underground . . .
  "Steven! Oh. I don't usually do this. But I've never met anyone like you.
Ever. Here's my address and phone number. If you're ever in L.A.—"
  "I'm sorry, I'm married—with children. I'm flattered, but I can't
reciprocate."
  "Oh. (*Pause*) Well, if you're ever in L.A. . . . I'll be staying at the Hilton
'til Friday."
  I took the show ticket with his name and address, "Thanks."
  After I saw my manager, I walked back to the parking garage. And
like a good husband, I tore up that ticket, hopped in the mini-van, and
high-tailed it back to Connecticut!
  And on the Merritt Parkway, I couldn't stop thinking about him. Fan-
tasizing. Blown away at his response. This seemed to be happening to
me all the time. It was following me wherever I went. I was tormented.
Why wouldn't it leave me alone? I wasn't cruising. I just wanted to see a
matinee. "No! I do not want to be gay!" I hit the steering wheel. "No! No!
Why me? No! No! No! *I do not want to do this to my family!*"
  I got home late. Emily was cold to me and went upstairs. I was so
lonely. "I just need good friends. That's all he has to be!" So I stayed
downstairs and called every Hilton in Manhattan—'til I found him. We
just talked about Shakespeare. *As You Like It.* But I had crossed the line.
We started corresponding . . .

✐

And about this time, I stopped smiling. And when I looked at
Emily, I noticed she'd stopped smiling, too. And when I thought about
it, she hadn't smiled for a long time. Since maybe even our honeymoon.
She'd shut down.

What did she want to say but couldn't? Besides giving up a promising career, was it the loneliness of being a grad-school widow with the accompanying poverty? The chaos of Fisher-Price plastic scattered everywhere and the sleep deprivation that comes with two small children? Don't all couples get married this young and lose their sexual spontaneity after kids? Or was it that she had married her father?

After almost seven years together, though we had photo albums filled with great times (and we threw the best Mormon parties!), the realities of what we had really taken on were finally starting to set in. We were too afraid to admit the truth. We were in so deep. So we kept pretending. Pretending to be a perfect, straight Mormon couple. (*Smiles while speak-singing through clenched teeth*) It's ex-*haus*-ting!

But our hardships were nothing like what the early Mormon pioneers had to endure. Grit was in our genes! My father used to say, "Who does the hard thing? He who can! Feel the pain, and do it anyway!" And the Church had taught us from a very early age to deny the pain and smile anyway:

(*Sings an LDS Primary Song.*)

> *If you chance to meet a frown*
> *Do not let it stay.*
> *Quickly turn it upside down*
> *And smile that frown away.* (*Smile fades on last word.*)

I believed the scripture in *The Book of Mormon*:
(*Reads*)

"And if men come unto me I will show them their weakness—and if they humble themselves before me, and have faith in me, then will I make weak things become strong unto them."

I was just weak. *But I could be strong!*

I decided to give it everything I had and threw myself back into reparative therapy. I felt I'd just put a Band-Aid on the issue and it was now time to buckle down and eradicate it once and for all. I broke all ties with that dirty blond I met in New York and went shopping for the best possible reparative therapist.

The theory behind reparative therapy (or conversion therapy) was that homosexuality was caused by an overbearing mother and a failed relationship with an emotionally absent father resulting in an impaired sense of masculine identity. By developing close friendships with salient, straight men, masculinity would increase and the "reparative" drive to fill the masculine deficit by merging sexually with another man would decrease or disappear altogether. This wasn't the aversion shock therapy of the past. This was the real deal!

I looked in the back of a guide put out by Focus on the Family called "Setting the Record Straight." It listed the National Association of Research and Therapy of Homosexuality or "NARTH." I called the number in California and they gave me a list of psychologists in my area that administered the kind of therapy I was looking for. (What they didn't say was that the American Psychological Association deemed it harmful and unethical.) After interviewing in person with three local therapists, I decided to do phone therapy with the president of NARTH himself. I liked his Brooklyn accent and his gay jokes. I was willing to do or say whatever he wanted me to. The cure would only cost me the long-distance phone bill and $135 per 45-minute session.

It came down to pay for therapy or rent. My insurance (and my physician father) wouldn't cover it, so I finally broke down and went to the bishop. "I'd been paying tithing and fast offerings my whole life. Could the Church please help me pay for this therapy to prevent me from turning gay and to keep my Forever Family together?" He didn't know much at all about what I was dealing with. So I bought him books about the ex–gay movement to educate him. He never asked how it was going. He just cut the checks.

I was seeing my Catholic phone therapist (twice a week) under the sound science of NARTH. Under his direction I wrote a letter to my mother blaming her for my homosexuality. I told her not only to stay out of my life, but my son's as well. I was afraid she was going to turn my son gay, too! He couldn't figure out why his beloved Grandma Butterfly didn't call or come to see us anymore.

He gave me a list of books to read. Some of the books were so painful that I'd find myself falling asleep after each chapter to escape. One book said that real men shouldn't drink sissy drinks—that you should have hard liquor on the rocks. I didn't even drink Coca-Cola.

I also re-read the Church's seminal writings on sin, *The Miracle of Forgiveness*. In the chapter on the "sin next to murder" it quoted an ancient Greek philosopher: "The first and greatest victory is to conquer yourself; to be conquered by yourself is of all things most shameful and vile." The philosopher was *Plato*.

I then joined HOPE, an Evangelical Christian ex-gay men's support group in Massachusetts. I'd drive two and a half hours to witness all these married men sitting around overcoming their same-sex attraction—together. I never missed a meeting.

Above all I needed to build straight, salient male friendships. I was the church home-teacher to a man who was a football coach at UConn. He didn't know it yet, but he was going to be my "salient male." One night I just popped over, like good home-teachers do, to see if he needed anything from the Church or if I could do anything for his family. He was watching *Plays of the Day* on ESPN. We just sat there and watched . . . and watched . . . and watched as I waited . . . and waited . . . and waited to turn straight.

My therapist suggested I go to this weekend warrior retreat in New Hope, Pennsylvania. You know, men denouncing their mothers as they hug trees and beat drums in the forest. At the end they held this initiation ceremony. It was a freezing cold February night as they led me and the others blindfolded from outside into this log cabin. I could smell the sage smoke. There was all this chanting. When they took off my blindfold, there was every man that had ever taken the course dancing around this bonfire—*naked*! All kinds of body types had come from far and wide to initiate us. I was called up before the chief. I was stripped of my clothes. There I stood as he handed me two oranges and gave me a new name: Buck! As we went in the sweat lodge, they all congratulated me on getting my balls back.

I rubbed shoulders with my Priesthood Elders Quorum on Sundays. Everything was financed by Mormon money.

You see, it takes a village to make one straight.

I was on my way to heterosexual wholeness! So I flew to my closet, and I threw anything out that might fit tightly or was pink or purple. I turned a blind queer eye and stopped taking an interest in any activity or skill that had a gay association. I stopped working out so I wouldn't be attracted to men doing squats at the gym. And I stopped watching the Lifetime Channel. I started listening to Garth Brooks and George Strait instead of Ricky Martin or "Bernadette Peters at Carnegie Hall." I uncrossed my legs and lowered my voice. Steven became *Steve.* "Right on. (*Wipes nose on sleeve*) It's all good, dude." I was becoming this tightly coiled, homophobic homosexual. With no sense of humor. If anything I was becoming asexual.

They said *this* was my true self. But doesn't your true self smile? And shouldn't your true self find your stunning wife or any woman arousing? And why was I now having vivid homoerotic dreams? After all the time and money and energy, I still had to fantasize about a man to ejaculate while making love to my wife. That was our reality. The therapy wasn't helping. We both knew it. We didn't talk about it. We just pressed forward. And I took my temple marriage covenants seriously. Especially when I looked at our kids. We were a *Forever* Family, right? (*Pause*) We did smile when we looked at them . . .

∽

One day, driving home from another pointless open-call in New York, I heard this voice:

VOICEOVER: "Steven, you could move back to Utah and keep your family together, and you might actually like it."

"But I want to be in a big Cameron MacIntosh musical! *Phantom* or *Les Miz . . . 'Meow?'*"

As head of the house and patriarch of my home, I decided we should move. I hadn't had sex outside my marriage, but I felt I was a walking time bomb. Was it only a matter of time before it would all blow up? I didn't want it to blow up on Emily on the East Coast where we didn't have any family. In my head I was confident and optimistic that I could keep it all together. But in my heart I knew I was only postponing the inevitable.

I decided my mother wasn't to blame. *Acting* was the culprit. Working in the theatre and commuting to New York presented many hazards to my eternal salvation. The male dancers in tights at auditions began to look intriguing, the porn shops on Eighth Avenue—inviting. So I decided to just take myself out of the situation entirely and move to where none of that existed—Salt Lake City! (Where Jews are considered gentiles.)

It was time to show God (and Emily) just how serious I was about being straight. I'd sacrifice my dreams of Broadway. I wrote a song and we sang it as a family as we put on our smiles, loaded up the U-Haul and took our exodus across the country. We were goin' home. To the land of green Jell-O, "the everlasting hills", "the crossroads of the West", "the city of the Saints"—Zion!

(*Singing "You and Utah" while driving*)

> *I'm goin' home to Utah.*
> *I've gotta find my soul.*
> *I'm goin' where the girls are real*
> *And the men are whole.*
> *I'm goin' where the sun shines high*
> *And a cowboy can be true.*
> *I'm goin' home to Utah*
> *And I'm comin' home to you.*
>
> *I miss the Rocky Mountains.*
> *There's nothin' quite as tall.*
> *And summer wild flowers—*
> *Aspens in the fall.*
> *But most of all I miss your touch*
> *And the wonder of your smile.*
> *A life with you in Utah*
> *Is really more my style.*
>
> *Utah and me and you.*
> *Utah and you and me.*

I'll trade these lights for stars.
Trade your kisses for these scars.
There's no question now
What I should do.

You and Utah,
You never let me down.
Oh! You are all the reason I need
For leavin' this old town.
Don't you worry—
I'm gonna see this through.
Just stay right there in Utah.
A life with you in Utah—

I sang that song over and over again to convince myself that moving was the right thing to do. Utah was gonna solve all our problems. Utah was *not* going to let us down!

We got there—and I hated it. I loved the mountains and seeing Emily so happy. But I was miserable. *(Singing) "I'm so depressed in Utah, I think I've sold my soul."* I'd been away too long. I wasn't perfect anymore. I was a Democrat.

The first thing I did when we got to Utah, after finding a decent apartment for my little family, was to join Evergreen International. That's the official unofficial ministry for gay Mormons. I wanted to start associating with other strugglers who belonged to the "true church." They should call it EverQueen. I had never seen more rainbows, earrings, or tight jeans in my life! I volunteered to play the piano for the opening hymn and we had a devotional on sexual addiction. Then we divided into groups where everyone told their titillating stories of sex-behind-their-wife's-back that week. A hunky guy in short shorts came sauntering into the room late. This other guy leaned over to me and said, "Last time he was here he was caught giving this other guy a blow job right here on the church grounds!" I left the meeting disgusted, alone, and vowed never to return. I was far too advanced in my recovery for this crowd. And way too busy to join their basketball team.

The annual NARTH convention got too many threats to be held in Los

Angeles, so last minute it was being held in Salt Lake City. "Go straight. Go NARTH!" I wanted to be their poster child. I was asked to be a panelist on men who had overcome their same-sex attraction. Dr. Laura was going to be accepting an award. When I saw my beloved phone therapist for the first time I went over to him and touched his arm.

"Hi, Doctor. I'm Steve Fales."

"Uh, hello. You look skinny."

I was pale *and* skinny. I looked and felt ten years older than I was.

I introduced him to my wife (and a friend of hers) who had reluctantly come with me. He looked impressed and joked, "Are these your wives?"

That's all the time he seemed to have for me.

During my last long-distance session, after he told me how much pathology was associated with my condition, how he'd walked out of *Tea with Mussolini* because he didn't like Cher, and how Matthew Shepard was getting far too much attention, my beloved phone therapist said, "Remember Fales, you can put your penis where there's life or death. You'll never be happy with another man."

"Yeah, I know."

"Now that you're on track, we need you to help with the Cause. We need men who have succeeded in therapy to take part in this study that's tryin' to discredit our work. Don't tell them *we* referred you. Just tell them you heard about the study from . . . a *friend*."

I wanted to be NARTH's poster child. To make even Dr. Laura proud! My testimonial would be one of many used to prove just how pathological homosexuality is. It should've never been dismissed from the list of psychological disorders in the first place. The Gay Rights Movement would be stopped, starting with me!

So I called this enemy doctor in New York. He asked me all these questions. I told him all the *right* answers, inflating the truth when necessary. Then he asked me, "Do you feel isolated?"

"Of course not. Maybe if I lived in Chelsea or on the Castro . . . " But I was lying. I was isolated in Zion. I had never felt more alone in my life. I can't tell you what it cost me to lie . . . and smile.

So I had a choice to make. The ancient Greeks said, "Know thyself." Shakespeare said, "To thine own self be true." And in the sacred, secret Mormon temple ceremony it said that "through their *experience* they will come to *know*." Hadn't I come to Earth to find out who I was by gaining experience? Not avoiding it? I was tired of theorizing and philosophizing. I had to *viscerally* know who I was. I chose knowledge—like Eve. Ignorance fell from mine eyes as I waited to be cast out of the Garden. I partook of the fruit . . . and it was pretty dang tasty.

∽

After we'd lived in Utah almost a year, we finally got in a house in a nice suburb of Salt Lake. We fixed it up nice—mature blossoming cherry trees in the backyard. But as I scraped off the wallpaper and popcorn ceilings and painted and pulled out overgrown bushes, with every brushstroke, every repair, every shovel of dirt, I knew I was not going to be living there for long. But I wanted the house to be nice for Emily. She at least deserved that. And I especially wanted things to be nice for my kids. I wanted them to have a place they could be proud to bring their friends home to play.

Early one Sunday morning, after we'd lived in our new house about two months, I had an epiphany. And I wanted to articulate it to myself by writing an email to a confidant who had been a sounding board.

I went downstairs to the basement where the computer was and entered my password, "H-E-L-P."

(Typing)

"Sometimes I think I can have it all, but I'm finding I'm not a very good actor offstage. I think Emily suspects something is going on. The strange incoming calls on my cell, all the closing shifts at the restaurant, and you won't believe this, but she found the condoms in my bag when I got back from that trip to New York. He was this hot guy I met at 'Splash'!

I've been experimenting with this 'gay thing.' It's amazing that after sex with a guy, we can talk and talk. I've discovered moments where the kissing and full expression of who I am makes me feel so complete, so natural. It's not just about sex. It's an intimacy, an expression of my whole soul. It's been about an emotional/spiritual connection from the beginning.

You wouldn't believe how many married gay men there are here in Utah! I meet them on this local gay phone line. But it's got to stop. Now that I've had my masculinity validated many times (especially by that hot doctor with the Porsche that looked like Tarzan that thought *I* was so masculine!), I don't have the drive I did to have sex with men. The attraction to have sex with men may always be there, but now maybe it won't be as strong? I think I'm going to be able to be true to my wife now. Sex with her will have to be enough. Not as exciting and passionate, but fulfilling.... I've been true to myself the past six months, and the result is I may never need to 'act out' again. I think I'm going to be able to keep my family together and keep a smile on my face. I think I've faced my—"

"Who are you writing to, Steven?"
I shut off the monitor.
"No one."
"Are you having an affair?"
I couldn't lie anymore.
"Yes."
"With whom?"
"Several."
"How many men?"
"Twenty."
"It's over, Steven. *(Pause) It's over!*"
Emily wailed through the house and went to church alone.
I cracked—at thirty. Maybe if my paycheck came from the Church, or I had a huge Mormon estate or family name to protect, I could have stayed in the box a little bit longer. But I finally cracked.
I hadn't had intercourse with twenty men. Most of the time it was just fooling around and some were repeats. I hadn't fallen in love with anyone—yet. But I *had* committed adultery. I'm not proud of that. Or the fact that no matter how safe I thought I was being, I was putting my wife at risk for a disease that had killed her father. So to show Emily I was repentant (so I wouldn't lose her and the kids), I turned myself in—again.

"Hi, Bishop. Sorry to call you so late. It's Brother Fales. *Fales.* We shook hands once at church ... I've been unfaithful. And it hasn't been with a woman. Get a blood test? Okay. Sure. I can meet you tomorrow. Two o'clock? See you then."

The bishop took time out from work to meet me at his office. He was a sincere man with white hair, a kind round face, and glasses—kinda like Santa Claus. "Brother Steven ... We all have something in this life that we have to overcome. I deal with swearing."

After he finished, he stopped me and pointed to this picture of Christ on the wall—handsome, rugged, all-American. (I call it the "Mel Gibson Jesus".) "I like this picture of Jesus because He's not portrayed as some waifish, poetic wimp. We should all look to *this* Jesus for guidance." The bishop and I go for the same type!

I was then sent on to the next ecclesiastical leader—the stake president. A bishop presides over a ward, many wards make up a stake (like a diocese) presided by the stake president. Now if you're a serious sinner like me, the sin against nature herself—he takes over. Kinda like the Feds taking over for the local sheriff. It's a pretty big deal. The stake president represents Christ himself and has the keys to bind or loosen all my blessings and covenants. He had the authority to blot my name out on earth and heaven.

I remember walking into the painted cinderblock stake presidency wing of the stake center next door (one of the conveniences of living in Utah!). I checked in with the executive secretary who sat behind the glass. It felt so clinical. I couldn't believe it was actually me sitting there. Would I be *excommunicated*? And wasn't excommunication for the *wicked*? How had I come to this? I had only ever wanted to be a good boy and do what was right. When I was little I used to tell my Aunt Linda, "I just feel Heavenly Father with me all the time."

It used to be you'd be excommunicated for just having homosexual feelings. I had taken it quite a bit further. If I were "ex'd", I'd become like any non-member. Only worse, having been one of the elect and sinned against the Greater Light, that would bring greater consequences. I wouldn't be allowed to take the sacrament, pay tithing, or pray or sing in church again. The Holy Ghost would no longer be with me. And beyond this, I would be barred from seeing my children in the afterlife.

Memories of my years of church participation flooded me. Like most Mormons, church was my life. Getting baptized by my dad when I was eight. Getting blessings from him when I was sick. Passing the sacrament to my mother for the first time when I was twelve in my new white shirt and tie. Ward Christmas parties, stake road shows, scouting and church sports, youth dances and firesides. Good times! *Good people.*

And the temple. Everyone dressed in white. I loved just sitting in the chapel listening to the hymns played on the organ, or praying in the Celestial Room. Quiet. Peaceful. Holy. *"Holiness to the Lord."* I believed it with all my heart. And every dream I'd ever had was centered around the Church ...

(Recording plays of a child singing "I Wonder When He Comes Again")

(The child on the recording breaks down in sobs and stops singing. Steven joins in, taking over for the child and finishes the song a cappella.*)*

I wonder when He comes again,
Will herald angels sing?
Will earth be white with drifted
snow?
Or will the world know spring?
I wonder if one star will shine
Far brighter than the rest.
Will daylight stay the whole night
through?
Will songbirds leave their nest?
I'm sure He'll call His little ones
Together 'round his knee.
Because He said in days gone by,
"Suffer them to come to—"

I especially loved the Primary songs I learned as a kid. Primary's like Catechism. I loved singing in church! When I was little, my mom used to play for me as I'd sing at all kinds of church meetings. This is me. I was nine years old here. This was one of my favorite songs. I sang it all the time. I even sang it once for "Show and Tell" in kindergarten. This was recorded at my cousin Joshua's funeral. He drowned. He was only two.

Just then the stake president opened his office door and stepped out. The bishop said I'd really like him.

"You must be Brother Fales? *Welcome.* It must be very difficult for you to be here. Thank you for coming. *The Lord loves you." (Pause)*

That's what I *imagined* him saying. What I got was, "Now what's your name?" I was stunned. I was the only one there. Surely my name was on his Franklin Covey planner. Was I one of dozens of neighborhood homosexuals he was seeing that day? Would he have forgotten my name if I were a client at work or a potential new convert?

"Brother Fales."

I went in his office and sat down.

"I can't believe you didn't know my name. Do you even know why I'm here?"

"Yes, I know why you're *here."*

It was a little thing, not knowing my name. But for me, it was huge. It summed up my whole experience growing up in the Church. I always felt I needed to win the Brethren's approval. I wanted them to like me. I wanted to be like them. To be noticed. *I was invisible.* No matter what I did or how well I did it, I felt I was never accepted or appreciated for who I was. I felt I knew what it must be like to be a woman in this church.

We didn't start off well. The usual opening prayer was *not* offered and he asked me to define sin. How did I feel about sin? Did I *think* I had sinned? We weren't getting anywhere. I didn't have the right answers anymore. My absolutes were failing me. I couldn't say what he needed or wanted to hear.

"*Mister* Stake President. It's been doctrine this and dogma that my whole life. Work, work, work out your salvation! Never being worthy enough of God's love! *Where is the love?"*

He told me they needed to keep the Church "*pure."*

I told him the Church was a "*socio-economic-political-tax-exempt-multi-national-corporation posing as the Kingdom of God on Earth."* (Pause) It just came out!

He wanted to have the Church Court right away.

✑

The Sunday before my Church Court, I skipped the rest of the three-hour block of meetings and went home after Sacrament. I guess for once I just didn't feel like sitting through another Priesthood lesson on home-teaching and the importance of a one-year supply of food storage. I turned on the TV. PBS on Church-owned KBYU. Goody! There was a special on about the American Revolution. They were talking about Benjamin Franklin and how much he had loved England. I never knew this, but he tried over and over again to keep the peace, to resolve the differences between the mother country and the angry colonists. He was loyal to England. But the taxes kept getting higher and higher. Abuse after abuse ensued. Finally, Benjamin Franklin joined his brothers in the Revolution. He found himself at war with the country he had loved and served his entire life—the country of his birth. I was beginning to see how much Ben and I had in common. I was at odds with the *church* of my birth. We were both reluctant revolutionaries.

My Church Court was set for the next Sunday at 7:00 A.M.

(Begins putting on a white shirt, tie, and suit jacket.)

It was the middle of July. I was working two jobs, re-painting the house, writing a new Mormon musical, preparing to throw a big birthday bash for my wife, and in all my spare time I was "Daddy." And in the midst of everything my Church membership and my marriage were at stake.

No! My marriage wasn't just at stake. It was over. I had never seen Emily with such resolve! And as loving as her mother was to me, Carol Lynn was pressing her daughter hard to end this marriage immediately. It was clear I was going into this with everything to lose—including salvation.

Mormon men are supposed to be clean-shaven. I had just played Perchik in *Fiddler on the Roof* at Robert Redford's Sundance Summer Theatre the night before. (Perchik's the socialist who starts all the trouble by dancing at the wedding!) That's why I had a beard at the time. Not the best way to make a good first impression.

In some ways it's like attending your own funeral. I put on my Sunday best and was ready when the bishop came by to accompany me to my disciplinary council. Or "Court of Love", as they call it. I was "calm as a summer's morn" as I went like a "lamb to the slaughter."

When the high councilmen all arrived (the grand jury), I was led into the room. There must have been about twenty men all dressed in dark suits and power ties. They all rose. *No one was smiling.* I thought, "Now *this* is the way to get a straight man's attention!"

They led me to the head of this enormous oak table where I sat next to the stake president. He had the secretary read the charge: "HOMO-SEXUALITY." I was surprised they used that word. Hadn't I been "immoral" or committed adultery? Wasn't that why I had turned myself in and everyone was there? Then they turned the time over to me, the guest of honor. I was allowed to tell these men, whom I had never seen before, my story.

I told them. *Everything.* I spoke my truth. One brother fell asleep. Another checked his watch. They did have many other church meetings ahead of them.

After I finished, they wanted to ask me a few final questions.

"*What was my most spiritual experience?* My wedding day. Kneeling across the altar with Emily. I'd been crying throughout the whole thing. I felt God had given me such a precious gift. Who else would marry a gay man? I never wanted to hurt her. I intended to be with her forever."

"*Is being in the arts causing my homosexuality?* I only sleep with doctors, lawyers, and cowboys—never other actors."

"*Have I ever had sex with a minor?* No! I'm into *men*."

"*Have I ever sexually abused my son?*" I was as good a father as anyone in that room. Did they ask that question to straight men? Did they ask if they had ever sexually abused their daughters? I looked them right in the eye, "No."

I was then asked to leave the room so they could discuss and pray.

Mormonism is the fastest growing religion in the Western Hemisphere. Church membership has more than doubled in my lifetime. With over twelve million members, I was expendable. I knew they were not trying to talk Emily into working things out. The church welfare system would take care of any financial needs she had after the divorce. In this case, divorce certainly seemed justified. And at the same time I knew some Church leader somewhere was counseling some gay young man to go ahead and get married. Another daughter in Zion would be sacrificed to straighten her husband out. And when would the next teenager come home after a Sodom and Gomorrah lesson in church or seminary and try to commit suicide? Or run away to be a porn star in Palm Springs?

VOICEOVER: "Brothers and Sisters: When the spiritual death is total, it were better that such a man were never born."

They brought me back after ten minutes. And the stake president said they had decided to . . . excommunicate me. And then he proceeded to pronounce my sentence in a formal declaration they are required to read to everyone. I just folded my arms, closed my eyes, and bowed my head. His voice became full and resonant:

VOICEOVER: "Brother Fales: This is the Church of Jesus Christ of Latter-day Saints. It is the Kingdom of God on Earth. Because you have transgressed—"

I can't remember all that was said. I just remember how I *felt*. And I wasn't expecting to feel this way. His voice faded out, as this warm feeling of peace and truth washed over me as another Voice said, "*Steven, I know who you are. And I am so much bigger than this church . . .*" (*Pause*)

When it was over (it took three hours), the high councilmen all lined up at the door to shake my hand. I'd just been kicked out of the Church, yet they were all smiles and eager to wish me good luck. One brother gave me a big hug and said I was going to be "okay!" Another brother just shook my hand and sobbed. I noticed he'd been crying throughout the whole Church Court. I couldn't help wondering why.

As I exited the high council room and stepped into the hall, I noticed Sacrament Meeting was just beginning in the chapel for one of several wards that shared the church meeting house. The congregation was singing full-throttle. I stopped to listen for a moment, then slipped quietly out the back of the building into the bright summer day and walked home.

That night I slept again in the basement. And I just basked in the warm glow of that Voice. And that night, I had a dream:

I dreamed I was on the family farm in Wyoming where my father grew up. There the land is flat, except for Heart Mountain standing alone like a bear tooth in the distance. A harsh, dry country where summer is short and crops of sugar beets and pinto beans need irrigation to survive. I walked into this abandoned barn filled with cobwebs. In the corner was this dusty wooden chest filled with tack: saddles, halters, leather bridles. I opened the chest and picked up one of the reins and instantly found myself riding across the high desert plains on horseback.

My horse was magnificent! We were galloping at this exhilarating pace. I soon noticed I was joined by my father on his horse, and my grandpa on his, and his father, and his father's father. And soon I was riding with multitudes of my ancestors, racing ahead, leaving a dust cloud behind us that extended for miles. I didn't know where we were going or why we were going so fast, but it felt amazing to be part of this family of fathers and sons all united with this incredible sense of urgency to get *somewhere*—

I woke up! I didn't know where I was headed. But maybe I was gonna be okay. And the warm feeling of that Voice continued throughout the entire week. Until the letter from the Church declaring me officially excommunicated came in the mail.

There it was in black and white. I was excommunicated for "homosexuality." The letter was so *nice*. But I got so angry. And I couldn't figure out why. Then I realized it was because I was excommunicated for something the Church said didn't exist:

VOICEOVER: "Brothers and Sisters: The words 'homosexual,' 'lesbian,' and 'gay' are adjectives. Refrain from using these words as nouns. That would imply that a person is consigned to a circumstance in which he or she has no choice."

I wasn't tried for adultery or immorality or heresy or just wanting someone male to hold me in his arms. I was excommunicated for a small but quintessential part of who I *am*. Even after all the things I'd done to change. As they promised I could! I'm not just an adjective. *I'm a noun*.

I thought about suing for malpractice. But how do you tell God his chosen, anointed servant has his parts of speech mixed up? And though they said I could be re-baptized in a year if I fully repented, I knew I could no longer be part of their *esprit de corps* because I refused to check my individuality and common sense at the chapel door.

∽

But I'd rather be excommunicated a thousand times than have to repeat the day we told our children we were getting divorced. It was Emily, our daughter, our son, and me. I didn't know how to explain something like this, but I was still the dad so I felt it was my duty to break the news. They were too young to know everything, and yet I didn't want to blow it off like nothing was happening. I knew from experience what it felt like to have your parents break up.

I was sixteen when they divorced. There were many reasons for this, but I'll simply say that my parents were extreme opposites. My mother would rather eat *foie gras* and lobster than pay for insurance. My dad would let us starve before he missed a premium—and didn't know what "foy grass" was. To many we were the perfect Mormon family. Our entire stake was devastated and my world was shattered when they split. The performing arts saved my emotional life.

So I decided to make the incision swift and clean.

"Mommy and Daddy are getting divorced."

My son's head shot to attention. He was only five but he knew exactly what that meant. "No. No? *No!*" He ran to his room, putting his hands over his ears. Em and I followed. He was in there praying. "Please, Heavenly Father. No! They'll ruin my life! They'll ruin my life! *No! No! No! No! No!*" He was echoing the same words I yelled as I hit my steering wheel in my Gethsemane on the Merritt Parkway.

As the divorce got closer, I got confused and scared. I didn't know how to be alone. And I didn't want to give up "hugging time".

You see, Emily and I shared a tradition her parents started. You know how early kids wake up? Well, we'd try to sleep in—putting off their needs as long as we could. Then when we couldn't do it any longer we'd yell out, "HUGGING TIME!" In our two kids would run and jump on the bed. We'd hug and kiss and snuggle—all warm and safe and happy. Couldn't I give it all up for the sake of "hugging time"? I didn't know what I wanted, but I was going to fight for "hugging time"!

I turned it all on Emily. It was her fault. *She* never wore enough lingerie. *She* wouldn't watch the *Better Straight Sex* videos I ordered from the back of *GQ*. Emily knew going into this marriage it might finally come to this, and now that I've finally cracked, she's just going to throw me out? How dare she watch *Will & Grace* and laugh when I was trying to change. She had failed *me*!

It was all happening too fast! I got in touch with the church's main psychologist.

"Steven, if I could just lower your I.Q. by ten points and Emily's emotional I.Q. by ten points, I could save this marriage."

He said I could still change!

"Go ahead, Emily. Go be single like your mother. Go be *Carol Lynn Pearson*. You've got blood on your hands. I want to work this out. You are just a wimp!"

When I refused to sign she threatened me with alimony. I hurried to the bank to have my signature notarized and ran back to where the kids were in the middle of swimming lessons. I thrust the papers at Emily.

"Anything I ever do will come second to loving you!"

I gave her *sole* custody. Emily was afraid I'd try to keep the kids from growing up in the Church. I had no money to fight and I was outnumbered on all sides and completely beaten down.

But I didn't want my kids to miss me, so I left as many things as I could. And I planted daffodil bulbs (my favorite) all over the yard so in the spring they would come up, and my kids would hopefully feel my presence.

We went on one more family outing before I moved out. The summer was ending as we went up to Sundance and rode the chair lift together. "That's Mt. Timpanogos! That's where you proposed to Mommy, right Daddy?"

When I finally moved out, Emily and the kids were away for the afternoon. As I shut the door, I just held onto the door knob. I couldn't take my hand off. I'd tried so hard. I wasn't straight enough. "Bless them. *Oh, bless them.*" When I took my hand off, I knew it was over.

Our divorce was easy. We didn't need an attorney. It cost $150 and it took only three weeks to process. Emily got the house, the mini-van, the prints, the piano, the furniture, our wedding gifts, the CD collection, all the books—all our mutual friends. I left with all the debt, child support, two suitcases, a box—and all the guilt. Emily had come to life in Utah, but I had to leave. Every day the spires of the temple and other icons of my youth would hauntingly whisper:

VOICEOVER: "No success can compensate for failure in the home."

Remember that dirty blond from California I met in New York? So did I! I'd white-ed his name out in my address book. I scratched through and could barely make out the number. Was a life in Beverly Hills my reward for all I'd been through?

"Hi! It's Steven!"

He seemed surprised, but glad to hear from me. I told him how I'd really felt about him when we first met. He seemed impressed with my honesty.

"Are you still available?"

"Steven, I'm flattered, but I'm seeing someone." (*Pause*)

I decided to stay in Salt Lake through the fall to help my kids' transition. So after Christmas, with a one-way ticket, sixty dollars in my pocket, my unexpressed anger, and my smile (*Smiles*)—I moved to New York City! "Hey, NYC! Validate me!"

(*Urban noise. Pumping techno music. Pulsing lights.*)

(*To crew in light and sound booth*) Hold on! Wait a minute!

(*Sound, music, and pulsing lights stop.*)

I need to get out of these clothes first.

When you change your life you have to change your clothes. Including your underwear. Well at least in my case. Because up until my excommunication, I wore my sacred temple priesthood garments—or magic Mormon underwear—day and night.

(*Starts to undress.*)

I remember my dad wearing them when I was a kid. Back when they were one piece with convenient special openings for when you needed to go to the bathroom. They are now more modern than the ones the pioneers wore that covered them wrist to ankle. My dad did nearly everything in them. I can picture him wearing them kneeling in morning prayer. I could have been conceived while he was wearing them.

Today they come in two pieces. Tops and bottoms. They come in all kinds of fabrics from cotton to polyester blends and have special markings that only temple-attending members know about. You have to buy them at specially designated outlets—kinda like a Kosher deli. They must never touch the ground. And when they get too worn out to wear, they have to be burned like an old American flag. They essentially look like T-shirts and really long boxers down to your knee. They only come in one color—white.

It's easy to recognize a Mormon male because the low scoop of the neckline of his garments shows under his white shirt. In Mormondom, it's jokingly called your "eternal" smile. In Utah, you need that smile not only to get into heaven, but to get a good job.

As a kid I anxiously awaited the day I'd become a super-duper orthodox Mormon like my dad, and go to the temple to get my garments. I was nineteen. Your garments become a "shield and a protection" to you—so long as you don't defile them. They help you resist temptation, avoid physical harm, and serve as a constant reminder to you that if you screw up you'll bring destruction upon yourself, "For God will not be mocked!"

(*Now just standing in white boxers.*)

So when they strip you of your Church membership, they strip you of your underwear.

(*Slips off white boxers revealing sexy black 2(×)ist briefs.*)

And they don't offer to buy you replacements. You're on your own. And the choices are overwhelming. Boxers, briefs ... for me, definitely briefs. But just how brief? And what does "two-times-x-to-the-i-s-t power *mean* anyway?" I can wear black now without fear. No one wears black in Utah ...

(*Sound, music, and lights resume. Steven gathers clothes and shoes and throws off-stage. Sound and music fade as he begins to dress onstage—all in black.*)

∞

My dad had just seen the movie *Billy Elliot*, and I think it made him feel guilty for making me pay for all my own voice and dance lessons in high school. So just before I left Happy Valley and went naked into "the lone and dreary world", my dad gave me a check to help me get on my feet and make all my dreams come true—*two hundred fifty dollars*. "Thanks a lot, Dad." I bought my plane ticket with it. And new underwear ...

I had a two-month sublet paid for, at least—a small, dark dive in Hell's Kitchen. I couldn't sit up in the loft-bed without hitting my head on the ceiling. I literally had sixty dollars in my pocket. That's thirty minutes in this town. How would I pay off my student loans, credit cards, old traffic tickets, child support? I needed new clothes, headshots, contact lenses. I didn't have insurance. How was I going to eat? Where would I workout? *When* would I see my kids again?

The energy of the city met me half way. Anything was possible!

My JetBlue flight arrived at JFK at 6:00 A.M. It was a Monday in the middle of January when I finally arrived in Manhattan. It was freezing cold, but I had a fire in my gut.

(*Music from* Evita *plays, "What's New Buenos Aires?"*)

"*What's new, New York City?* I'm from Utah! (*Salutes.*)" I hit the ground running—my Payless shoes killing me.

After I dropped off my luggage, I walked across Midtown to a posh French restaurant in the Seagram's Building to apply for a waiting job. A friend from grad school worked there and said he could hook me up. The manager interviewed me on the spot.

"I see you've worked at the *Macaroni Grill* ... ? But do you have any *New York* experience?"

"No. But I'm a really fast learner. *Really* fast." (*Smiles.*)

They started training me right away.

That afternoon I went to see an agent I'd been wooing long-distance for a few years.

"Would you be open to freelancing?"

"Sure. It's listed on my resume with all my other special skills."

"Would you be open to doing drinks later this week?"

"I think I can fit it in ... " (*Smiles.*)

He started sending out my headshot and resume right away.

It would be about two weeks before my waiting job would be bringing in any money. Auditioning doesn't pay. Subway tokens and slices of cheese pizza were getting really expensive. I began to panic, but was determined to survive. Later that night, I happened to pick up a free local gay rag and flipped to the back.

VOICEOVER: "Steven, here's an interesting, surefire way to make tons of money fast, *and* you might actually like it."

"You mean the job Mary Magdalene did before she met Jesus . . . ?"

I had an interview with one of the town's best male escort agencies— at midnight.

A male escort is usually hired by some middle-aged woman to help her out of her limo, walk her down a red carpet and then sit by her and hold her hand as they announce she's won some award. Not! An escort or "companion" is a hooker, a prostitute. Ninety-nine percent of the time you are hired for one thing if you are a man: gay sex.

I wasn't sure exactly what to do, but I was relatively new to gay sex, voraciously horny, and ten years behind. I needed technique. I might as well get paid for learning. I'd always been an overachiever. So I thought of it as a gay internship!

My new pimp was nice—much more normal than I expected. He didn't try to have sex with me or beat me up. No drugs. The apartment was warm and comfortable—Tiffany lamps. We talked about show biz and then *his* biz. And how many respected professionals had hustled to finance their educations, careers, dreams. He'd been an escort-slash-porn star in his early years and went on and on about his glory days, how much money he'd made, the apartment he'd bought. At one time he must have been the Belle of the Ball, but the lines on his face told me he'd had a few too many vodka and tonics and cigarettes in his not-so-distant youth.

"Everyone's a prostitute at one time or another. Do you think everyone likes their job? Even housewives put out for security. They're just paying for your time, remember. And furthermore, temple hookers were often considered sacred and holy in ancient times."

He needed to see how big I was before I filled out the W2s. So I pulled down my pants. "Nice!" And got the job.

"Thank you, Greek great-grandfather!"

I was to be billed as the new twenty-four-year-old versatile top from Utah with the Mormon manners and Donny Osmond smile. Elder Sodomite straight to your door and at your service.

(*Music from* Evita *plays,* "Don't Cry for Me, Argentina".)

> *Don't cry for me, Salt Lake City.*
> *The truth is I've found my calling.*
> *And if you thought that I was a sinner—*
> *You ain't seen* nothin'*!*

"I'll show you just how *gender-disoriented* I can be, Salt Lake. Oh! And, Dad? *(Pause) Watch me provide.*"

∽

The next night I was at the restaurant when the pager the agency gave me went off. I snuck over to the pay phone (since my cell phone had long been turned off), and called the agency. One of their best clients wanted to see me. After my shift I took the subway to Union Square, found the luxury apartment building, checked in with the doorman, and was sent right up.

When I got to the penthouse door, I took a deep breath and rang the bell. (*Doorbell ring*) What was I doing? I had never played *this* role before. As I clutched the strap of my backpack, I just thought about the money, seeing my kids again—"If you were helping me, *Dr. Dad*, I wouldn't have to be *doing this!*"

The door opened, I put on the smile and began to improvise. "Hi! I've got a message I'd like to share with you about non-traditional families. May I come in?"

He was this short, skinny, older Japanese man dressed in a black silk kimono.

"Uh, Jason?"

"Yes?"

"Oh, *Ja-son*. Ah, come in!"

(I used a different name when I worked.)

"Take shoes off!"

I took my Payless shoes off and complimented the spaciousness of his place, the post-modern Asian décor. Like a good courtesan, I walked over to the Steinway.

"Mind if I play? (*Mimes playing the piano to a classical recording*) How did they get this up here?"

After some green tea and a bit of *Claire de Lune*, he showed me to the bedroom.

Everything was just as the agency said—two large TVs playing porn, tapes piled to the ceiling. (*Porn music starts*) He started to kiss me. He had these lizard lips that clamped down on my tongue. I started to gag. Then he undid my pants and clamped down on my penis. Nothin' was movin' down there. *Nothin'*! Then I remembered what they told me at the agency, "Just watch the videos!" I couldn't take my eyes off! Thank goodness something started to move down there. So he reached over and grabbed a condom and some lube. And before I could lose my hard-on, he strapped poppers to his nose, bent over, and told me to "stick in now!" He couldn't get enough as I just kept watching the videos.

STEVEN: (*Topping a la ropin' cowboy*): Yeeeeeeee-haaaaaaaah!

LIZARD: (*Bottoming with Kamikaze-Suzuki yell*): Hai! Hai!! Hai!!! Hai!!!! Haiiiiiiiiiaaaaaaaaaaaaaaaaaaaaaah!!! (*Pause*) Hai.

He finally came.

I did *not*!

I excused myself to the bathroom. I rinsed off in the shower and borrowed some mouthwash. (I actually felt bad about not asking to use it.) When I came out, he was lying on the bed smoking a cigarette. "You good. *Leeearry* good!"

He gave me $350; I gave him (*Geisha bow*) . . . my smile. (*Smiles.*)

I was out the door ten minutes early and off in a taxi to pay the agency their cut, then off to the Roxy with mine. I was now off-duty. It was time to have fun . . . on *my* terms:

(Techno music pumps. Pulsing disco lights. The Roxy, a famous gay nightclub. Dancing wildly toward bar)

TO BARTENDER: "Please. Cosmopolitan? (*Tipping big*) Thank *you!*"
TO HOOK-UP: "Really? I bet you say that to all the girls. Hot yourself. Where do you work out? *Me, too!* Hi, Chuck. *Steve.* Miami? Salt Lake City. Hell's Kitchen. You? *Closer.* Shall we go?" (*Smiles*)

℘

My Japanese Lizard called me back the next three nights in a row! The agency said he'd never done *that* before. It was clear I was a natural. Definitely A-list material. Other calls immediately followed. And they weren't all trolls like the Lizard. Some johns were downright husband material—hot, young, professional, rich, mysteriously unattainable. Gramercy Park. Sutton Place. Park Avenue. Fifth Avenue. The Four Seasons. The Carlyle. As the penthouses got higher, so did the pile of cash and gifts on my dresser at home. The adoration and money made me high. I could fetch $500 an hour. $2,000 overnight. Tax-free! And if I arranged it all myself, I could keep it all. I traded in my Payless shoes for Prada:

(Escort montage. Each of the following "client scenes" takes place in a different sexual position. Various styles of music underscore each scene to ironic/comic effect.)

TO CLIENT A: "You know, I never thought I'd work for the Bush administration. D'ya know I used to be a Republican? Did you know Orrin Hatch is a Mormon? No, I've never been to the Hamptons or Fire Island. Tell me all about your place. Have you ever been to Park City?"

TO CLIENT B: "I *love* this CD. No way, you are not his manager! Did you know Gladys Knight's a Mormon? Wow! What an incredible view of Lincoln Center. I've never been to the Met. Could you take me backstage?"

TO CLIENT C: (*No music*): "So *this* is where the Security Council meets. Did you really address the Full Assembly? Reminds me of General

Conference at Temple Square. I love a powerful man in an Armani suit and tie."

TO CLIENT D: "You know, you really didn't need to send the limo. But I'm glad you did. And thanks for the new Tiffany cufflinks. And the cologne and sweater. Cashmere!"

TO CLIENT E: "This wine feels like silk going down. D'ya know, a year ago I didn't know a Merlot from a Chardonnay? Boy Scout's Honor!"

TO CLIENT F: "No worries, dude. Let's just kick it and see what we can make shoot all over. You like it nasty? You like this piggy Mormon Boy talkin' dirty to you, huh?"

TO CLIENT G: "What do you mean you just wanna talk? Okay. (*Sighs*) Alright, I can hold you. It's gonna be okay. I'm sorry your boyfriend left. But you're, like, sixty-five? And he's, what? Twenty?"

TO CLIENT H: "Pretasi sheets . . . Let me get you a warm washcloth. I'm glad you liked it. If they only made condoms for my heart—I'm so easily infected. How much do I need? I could use a new laptop. Five thousand? (*Snatches check. Then with absolute sincerity:*) Thank you."

My mercenary pioneer work ethic came in handy. But at the same time, money had no value. Giving a twenty here and there to a beggar each week was a heck of a lot cheaper than paying tithing. I even gave to Broadway Cares/Equity Fights AIDS. *I was* taught to care for the needy in Sunday School. I couldn't get *The Book of Mormon* out of my mind:

"For behold, are we not all beggars? Do we not all depend upon the same Being, even God, for all the substance which we have?"

(*Techno music. The Roxy again.*)

TO BARTENDER: *Aye! Aye! Aye! Corona con limón! Gracias!*
TO HOOK-UP: *Hola!* I bet you say that to all the *señoritas. Esteban.* Juão?

Oh! (Switching from Spanish to Portuguese) *Brasiliero?! Viva Brasil! Danca a Limbada! Sim! Eu falo Portugues! Eu fui um missionario da Igreja de Jesus Cristo dos Santos dos Ultimos Dias. Sou Mormon! Voce tambem? Muito bem.* Utah! (*Smiles*) *Vamos?*

❧

I found I'd rather be *eating foie gras* than serving it. So I quit my waiting job to start enjoying life a little. Oh, yeah. And focus on the acting career. I had my voice teacher, my singing coach, my acting classes, my trainer, my *affirmative* therapist. My legit theatrical agent started sending me out. I got callbacks for this and that Broadway show. I was offered an Off-Broadway contract—*Naked Boys Singing*. I auditioned just for fun, and getting naked at the dance callback wasn't as painful as I thought.

I turned the offer down—twice. I told my agent, "I didn't get an M.F.A. in acting to be naked eight shows a week." But the truth was I was a private dancer. I made more money in a call or two than an Off-Broadway contract paid in a week. More in a week than a Broadway contract paid in a month. Who needs Cameron MacIntosh?

So I decided to do Shakespeare—for free. Escorting could finance my art. I was cast as Prince Ferdinand in *The Tempest*, Off-off Broadway. I only had to take my shirt off in the second act, which appealed to my sense of Mormon modesty.

"Who are all the flowers from, Steven?"

"Oh, they're from a guy I'm dating. No, a different one."

(*Quoting Ferdinand in Shakespeare's* The Tempest):

> But you, O, you,
> So perfect and so peerless, are created
> Of every creature's best. Hear my soul speak:
> The very instant that I saw you did
> My heart fly to your service, there resides
> To make me slave to it and for your sake
> Am I this patient *log-man.*

I threw a lavish cast party in my new enormous Upper West Side sublet. I'm sure somebody must have wondered where I got the money to buy all that food and alcohol—and the cake with the image of the poster! "Fales is livin' large!" By non-union actor standards, my pad was a palace. But of course, I was a *union* actor now. I originally rented it because I wanted room for my children to come and stay—meanwhile, I thought I might as well entertain. And I did. In every room!

And my kids did come—in style! I invited my exiled mother to come fly out with them and spend Easter and her fiftieth birthday with us in New York City. When my mom and kids arrived in the taxi, I met them at the curb and hugged and kissed them. "How I loved just holding my children."

The poor dears had flown all night. When I got them upstairs and fed them in the breakfast nook (not to be confused with the large dining room) my daughter said, "Daddy, can we go to the top of the Statue of Little-bee?"

"Sure we can, sweetheart! You bet. *You bet!*"

And we did. We went to Central Park. Broadway shows—*The Lion King. Beauty and the Beast.* Shopping at GapKids. Serendipity. The Metropolitan Museum of Art (of which I was now a proud member!). I think my son would have preferred to go to a Yankees game. But that Jacqueline Kennedy exhibit was *not* to be missed! Who needs Disneyland when you can have the Big Apple? I pulled out all the stops. Especially for my mom.

It was time to pay her back for all the pain and suffering I'd ever caused, by throwing her a fiftieth birthday she would never forget. Spoiling her in ways her husbands wouldn't and only her gay son could! Her royal birthday treatment started with the first facial of her life followed by a massage and manicure and pedicure. Off to Macy's for an outfit. Then to Bergdorf Goodman to have her hair done and a makeover. I bought her all the products they recommended. She was radiant. She didn't look a day over forty. I hired an expensive Manhattan babysitter for the kids (I'd usually know some young woman in the ward to help out—but not this time). I bought a fancy birthday cake from Zabar's. We had a little with the kids and the sitter and were then off to the World Trade Center to have dinner at *Windows on the World.* The waiters treated her like a queen. They were tipped well for all the extras. How could I have written that cruel letter to her?

My sweet mom. My first Valentine! It was just like old times, we had such a fun time ripping on my dad!

Easter at *this* daddy's place was fabulous! I sent them home with new clothes and toys and a big fat check made out to Emily for child support.

When they left, I had to get right back to work. I was broke as you can imagine. And the Roxy wasn't cheap. Especially since I'd discovered ecstasy . . .

(*Techno music. The Roxy.*)

TO BARTENDER: Another Vodka and tonic. Now!
TO HOOK-UP, WITH MUCH LESS ENTHUSIASM THAN BEFORE.: I bet you say that to all the girls. Hi, Jeff. Steve. Miami? Salt Lake City. The 'W'? Love the 'W.' (*To another guy*) Shall we go?"

∽

I fell in love. He was just a little older and had been in New York a whole lot longer. He came from a fundamentalist Baptist background. He was an actor, though he hadn't worked in a while. He was a shirtless bartender and romance cover model now. We'd recite Shakespeare to each other by candlelight in my big sunken Roman tub with mirrors on three sides. And guess what? *He was an escort, too.* And *his* dad was a doctor!

"It's perfect! We can both work and then come home to each other. We can have it all! I'll arrange three-ways for us both."

But before long he didn't want to come home with me after work. He was too tired to hear about my kids.

"I'm falling in love with you."

"Baby, I am not what you need."

"Don't tell me what I need or who to fall in love with."

"Baby, I am doing this for your own good."

And he hung up! I kept calling back but he wouldn't answer or return my calls. Weeks went by:

(*Beep*) "Hey, stud. It's me—again. There's a guy coming up from D.C. We're seeing *Chicago*, then dinner, then back to his hotel. He wants two. And it's a thousand each. And you can bring your pot! (*Pause*) Look, I'm a little confused. I thought we really had a connection. You said you loved me. That you finally found someone who could understand. Or was that just the ecstasy talking . . . I don't let just anyone do what you did to me. So do give me a call, okay? Even if it's just to say you're too busy. Or you have a new boyfriend, or a husband, or a wife. *Give me a call, damn it. Ciao.*"

(*Techno music starts low and crescendoes.*)

"I gave up hugging time . . . for this? (*Pause*) NOOOOOOOO!!!!!"

(*Techno music stops.*)

I started working harder to forget about him. And as the calls came in, I couldn't say no. After all, I'd been trained my whole life to be nice and say, "Yes." I could do several calls in a day with the help of a little Viagra. And I got further and further away from auditioning. What was the point? I stopped seeing any real friends. Friends from graduate school or shows I'd done. My hours were screwy even by showbiz standards. And I couldn't tell anyone my secret—especially my family. Not to mention the new guy I started dating—each week. What would he think if he found out about my double life?

And about this time, I stopped smiling. Just selling my time, right? But I can't tell you what it cost me to sell my smile:

"I needed to win their approval. I wanted them to like me. I wanted to be like them. To be noticed. *I was invisible!* No matter what I did or how well I did it I felt I was never accepted or appreciated for who I was! I felt I knew what it must be like to be a—"

They didn't even know my name. I was more isolated now than I'd ever been in Zion. So I had a choice to make. (*Pause*) No. I was out of choices. I'd made too many.

(*Techno music. The Roxy.*)

TO BARTENDER: "Vodka—on the rocks!"
TO HOOK-UP: "Hey." (*Mouthing, "Ooo, yummy!"*)
TO BARTENDER: "TO GO!"

∽

I'd been escorting in New York for six months when a popular new movie came out, *Moulin Rouge*. I went to the Ziegfeld Theatre and watched it by myself. As I sat in the red plush chair, there up on the screen was Nicole Kidman (who really does look like Emily) playing this glamorous courtesan, a high-end prostitute—the star of the Moulin Rouge. I identified completely. She wanted to be a "real actress." And in her red dress she sang from her gilded elephant, *Someday I'll fly away. Leave all this to yesterday!*" "Truth, Beauty, Freedom, Love." When I took a close look at my new life, I didn't have any of these great "Bohemian" ideals the movie was championing.

By the end of the movie when Nicole finally dies of consumption, I was in emotional agony. Why was everyone around me enjoying the movie? "She's dying people! *I'm dying!*" I could see I was living my own personal *Moulin Rouge*. I'd had unprotected sex several times—not with clients, but on my own sexcapades. Was this knell tolling for me? What kind of person was I, jeopardizing my life like this? What kind of a father?

Voices of shame were screaming in my head. I had to get away from them—keep them quiet. So I went to the Roxy!

(*Techno music and lights.*)

"Come and get me boys!"
But this time, I couldn't seem to hook up. So I went home and I went online: UtahStudNYC@Do-Me-Now.com! And I found a group of guys with "PnP" profiles on Addicts Online who'd been partying all night and were looking for fresh meat. I arrived at their place in Chelsea at 5:00 A.M. They were doing a drug I'd only heard of—"Tina." *Crystal meth!* Something new to try. And before I knew it, I was doing rails of it, inhaling lines of vaporized speed as fast as they could heat it up. A little "G", a bump or two of "K" (*Super long snuff, then a long exhalation of imaginary white*

smoke), . . . and the voices were now quiet.

And I went out on the balcony. And there was the Empire State Building standing erect in the pink, cool summer morning light. And I wanted to sit on it. *And never get off.*

They were all set up for me. "Look, Dad. No condoms!" They showed me things and did things to me that I'd never imagined possible. And when it was over (*Primal grunt "Hunh!"*), I wanted MORE! But they kicked me out. So I found myself at a sex club. And I couldn't get enough there either. And when I ran out of cash, I forced myself to go home . . .

I checked my email. And with the crystal as my muse, I began to reply to a generous, sweet Waspy client who had fallen pathetically in love with me. He wanted to marry me! I had to break it off, I'd led him on too much. I was really not a good escort because I started to care about these people. The lines were blurring. I didn't know where my clients ended and my dates began.

I didn't know I could type this fast. Twelve hours and seven dense pages later I dropped the bomb. It's amazing how eloquent crystal makes you . . . and long winded! They don't call it speed for nothin'!

(*Reads paraphrase of letter.*)

I know that many would say that johns take advantage of escorts. These poor, wounded gay boys arrive daily in this city, running away in their pain, anger, and confusion from persecuting communities and disowning families. Many are using them. And sometimes they do offer help. But that is not what is happening here. I have been using *you.*

The number one job that an escort does, if he is good, is to make the client forget that the whole relationship is an illusion. That it's not a transaction. To make him feel that if the money wasn't there, we would still stay and care—so he'll keep coming back for more. You are a nice man. And I have hurt you. So I could get your money. I know better. And I'm sorry. I cannot see you again. I cannot love you back, like you would like. Thank you for the savings trust you created for my children. Please dissolve it.

All the best,
Steven

I hadn't had anything to eat in two days and started shaking. And crying. And shaking. And *crying*. I *couldn't* eat. I *couldn't* sleep. I couldn't even get off! So I started cleaning.

It was now going on three days. I thought I'd take a shower to try to clear my mind and clean off the sweat. I looked in the mirror. Was that *me*? I was so thin and pale, my face broken out. That pitiful, dilated, wild blank stare. I knew I had to tell someone what I was doing. I couldn't stand the isolation anymore. And the apartment was now clean!

"Please, God! Who do I call? Just give me a name!"

And the name came right to me in the shower, "*Steven, call your uncle John.*"

And I couldn't stop crying when he answered.

"John, I'm a prostitute! I think I'm HIV . . . !" (*Pause*)

He told me everything was gonna be all right—and that he wouldn't tell anyone. And I believed him enough to calm down, drink some Gatorade, and sleep . . . a little.

∽

The next day I resolved to stop escorting completely and went cold turkey. I called the agency and my clients and told them I was through. And I meant it! I hadn't saved any of the money I'd made, and it was all gone now, thanks to a new leather coat I bought in SoHo. I lived trick to trick. I'd planned to escort for at least another year—long enough to pay off my debts.

My new plan was to start writing—and modeling. Meanwhile I'd turn my apartment into a bed and breakfast. (I had four bedrooms.) I signed up to work with three catering companies. I even saw a committed relationship possible with some of the guys I was sleeping with. One was a plastic surgeon. One was a marine. One grew orchids. Before I didn't know where my clients ended and my dates began. (A boyfriend was anyone I'd slept with twice. And it's not that I was a slut—I just had a lot of boyfriends.) I'd talk to my kids on the phone and I put up the pictures they'd draw and send me. My smile was starting to come back.

Then September Eleventh hit.

No reservations were being made for my bed and breakfast. And I wouldn't be needed to cater. All parties were canceled.

My dad called! *But he didn't offer a dime to help me get by until things could get back to normal.* Modeling underwear *felt* like escorting. So once again I decided to survive—at all costs. I swallowed my pride and called the agency. They took me back in a New York minute. Lots of people needing to "connect", feel alive, not alone. War is big business! For weapon makers and *sex workers*. I wondered if I would ever smile again.

(*Techno music and disco lights. Steven mimes a handgun and slowly points to head.*)

VOICEOVER: "When the spiritual death is total, it were better that such a man were never born."

(*Phone rings.*)

"Hello?"

Old friends from Salt Lake. (That cool, non-LDS couple with three kids—Democrats.) They suggested I attend this *course*. (One of those three-day weekend courses that's supposed to change your life. Where everyone wears a nametag and suspiciously *smiles*.) They said they could arrange a scholarship. "Goody!" I had nothin' to lose. There wasn't a cult I hadn't tried . . .

The course started ridiculously early in the morning. I stumbled into the hotel ballroom—late. Over a hundred eager people sitting up tall. Beaming. Where was I? Church? "Gee, I hope I didn't miss the opening hymn!" I sat in the back. I turned my pager to vibrate, just in case a client called and I'd have to slip away.

The dynamic course leader, in her French accent (she talked just like 'zis!)—she brought up concepts like what it means to have *integrity*, to be *authentic* and *profoundly human*. Words like: *Transformation! Extraordinary! Possibility!* My pager went off! But I just kept listening. And before I knew it, I was under the Frenchwoman's spell as I began reexamining my life and belief systems. I couldn't stop thinking about my dad.

You see, my dad is cheap—*really* cheap. My whole *dang* life. If he loved me—*which he didn't!*—how could he be so cheap with me? Did I mention my dad is cheap? You'd think for having had my physician father be on call my whole life, I'd at least be compensated a little! Now, not only did he have a beautiful home in Vegas, but a ranch in southern Utah! And all those horses. You think he could sell one or two on my behalf. How many times had they kicked, stepped on, and bucked me off growing up?! During my parents' divorce, the judge gave my mother everything she wanted when it was uncovered that he spent more on his horses than his kids. Even the judge could see I was right! My dad hated me because of my career choice—and because I was born gay!

My *dad* was the reason my life was so crumby. Always roadblocking my success, sabotaging my happiness. I could never please him. He shamed me into getting married. He set me up. He gave me the name *Fales! Something* had to be done to get me out of my financial mess. It's my dad's fault I'm a whore. What else was I supposed to do? I was perfectly justified in doing what I was doing!

As I sat in my seat, Madame Course Leader had the audacity to suggest "'Zat my complaint was quite silly. It meant *nussing!* 'Zat my elaborate, entertaining, convincing little story" was just that—a story. One I'd actually invented?

And it hit me. *Hard.* She was right. I was crucifying my father for not being perfect so I didn't have to be accountable for my life. And to justify doing *whatever I wanted.* Wasn't the truth of it all, after my unique sob story was artfully told, that I thought I was special and an exception and the world should let me off the hook? Hadn't I bought into the idea that I shouldn't have to suffer and sacrifice and eat pasta and red sauce like all the other struggling artist/waiters in New York—because I was a poor gay Mormon who had kids? I had a history of jumping in too soon, biting off more than I could chew, and wanting it all perfect—*yesterday.* Didn't it all boil down to that? I was entitled and spoiled. Maybe I wasn't the singular sensation I thought I was?

Could I give up being "right" about my stories about the Church, therapists, the gay scene, Emily, her parents, my mother and especially my dad? *Could I stop being a victim?* Something deep inside me said, "*Yes!*" And in that moment, I was free. Free to choose. I had millions of choices! I was free to stop looking for my father's love and money in the penthouses of New York, free to stop self-destructing, and free to start cleaning up my messes . . .

So I called my father—at two in the morning.

And I told him. *Everything*. And I apologized for my disgusting behavior. And I told him that I thought he might love me. And that I loved *him*. And he'd demonstrated that in many generous ways (like providing clothing, food, shelter, braces—even paying for my mission and half of my undergraduate degree. With stepchildren and a new wife after a devastating divorce, he now had nine children to support!). After I began to list example after example of his generosity, and clearing several other important things up with him that are not expedient for me to tell at this time (no, he didn't sexually abuse me!), I asked him if we could please have a new relationship. And could he please forgive me for what I had done because I was so, so sorry. And he said he could! (*Pause*) And that he had always, *always loved me*.

So I called Emily—at three in the morning.

And I told her she was not responsible for my homosexuality. She deserved to have a man ravish her in the bedroom. To celebrate her femininity the way only a straight man could. She deserved her life back and to smile again. And could she please forgive me for cheating on her because I wanted to be her friend. And she said she wanted to hate me so bad, but that she couldn't and didn't. And after all that was said and done . . . *that I was a good father.*

And at the completion night of the course (where they tell you to bring as many friends as you can so that they can be "brainwashed", too), I wanted to share what I'd learned and "got" out of the weekend:

(*Harsh work lights come up on stage and in the house/audience, replacing theatrical lights. Steven steps down from the stage and into the aisle among the audience and re-introduces himself.*)

Hi. I'm Steven Fales. And I'm a Mormon. And that's why I smile like this. (*The smile is attempted, but now seems out of place like a useless old crutch.*) I'm an Eagle Scout. A returned missionary. I have two degrees. And two beautiful children. And I'm wearing a hairpiece. And I'll tell you why. My hair is thinning. And this piece makes me look younger, so I can compete with other escorts—and sleep with rich men for money. And I don't need it anymore.

(Steven efficiently removes his convincing, natural-looking hairpiece, which has been held on only with toupee clips and toupee tape. He is left "naked", revealing very fine, thinning hair.)

Because I'm not a boy. I'm a man. And I'm a dad. *(Pause)* I'm a dad!

(Work lights fade and theatrical lights resume.)

And once again I heard that now familiar Voice say, "*Steven, you're not anything you have ever done. And I still know who you are.*"

(Pause. He puts the hairpiece in his pocket where it stays the rest of the play.)

∽

I went down to the Public Health Clinic in Chelsea to get my free test results. When I got there the counselor said *(with an Hispanic accent)*:
"I'm sorry, yours are the only ones that isn't come back."
"That means I'm positive, doesn't it? They're retesting it because I'm positive!"
"Not necessarily. *Mira*, calm down! Come back tomorrow!"
That was the longest night of my life. I had to take two Excedrin PM just to knock me out. And that night, I had a dream.

Once again, I found myself riding across the scorching high desert plains on horseback—with all my forefathers. (Talk about a Marlboro ad!)
All of a sudden we came to an abrupt stop. Just a foot away was the deepest, widest gorge I'd ever seen. It reminded me of the Grand Canyon. It seemed a matter of life and death that we get across, but there seemed to be no possible way. Then one of the men, who seemed to have the authority to speak for the group, got off his horse and walked over to me.
"Son! Son, we need ya. We need ya to cry and fill this gorge so we can swim acrost. We gotta git there! We've worked and sweat our tears dry and have nothin' left. Will you fill this gorge for us?"

And so I did. I cried and cried, and the canyon filled with warm, sweet, salty tears—for sweat. Sweat for tears! We swam across. It was green on the other side. And there were my children . . .

The next day, I didn't have anyone to go with me to the clinic, so I took my favorite picture of my kids. I got on the subway and sat there holding them. I thought about Emily's dad, Gerald. My mind was racing out of control. I was desperately trying to make sense of everything as I prepared for the worst. Emily's father had never been to any of his kids' weddings. He had never seen his grandchildren. Would that happen to me? Who would tell my children and my grandchildren my story?

When I got to the clinic, I just stared in their beautiful, brown eyes. So much light shining back at me.

"Okay. What is it?!"

I was negative.

I ran home and fixed myself a humungous traditional Mormon family pot roast dinner with potatoes, carrots, and gravy (like my mother taught me how to make) to celebrate, and ate it by myself.

∽

At the Pier Dance (after my first Gay Pride Parade), I officially declared the end of my "gay adolescence." I couldn't believe how many of us there were. Thousands. Did God make this many mistakes? When it got dark, they set off the fireworks with the National Anthem playing. We all stopped to watch hand in hand—me and all my gay brothers and sisters. It felt so liberating to not have to be straight anymore. (Not that there's anything wrong with that.) Or to have to be a good Mormon. Or a good prostitute. (Not that there's anything wrong with that. Or that . . .) I just had to be human. And a good father. And someday, a good partner.

Though back home people thought I'd abandoned my family, I knew God knew that I was doing my best to smile and to see my kids as often as possible. (Thank goodness JetBlue flies to Salt Lake!) And what's so extraordinary was that Emily was not trying to keep them from me. I'm blessed to have my kids, and blessed that their mother loved her father (who just happened to be gay, too). In my heart I said a prayer. I thanked

God for my kids and Emily . . . and Gerald. Just then I got this impression to call Emily on my cell. Right there on the pier.

"Hi, Em. Em! Your dad wanted me to call you and wish you a happy Gay Pride."

"Thank you, Steven. (*Pause*) *Thank you.*"

∽

I was recently re-reading *Good-bye, I Love You* in Central Park. When I finished, I wept even harder than before. (An old woman who was sharing the bench with me got up and walked away, shaking her head.) What were we thinking? Except for the AIDS part, Emily and I had relived her parents' story, sometimes word for word—just on opposite coasts. Why did this have to happen? I take one look at our children, and I know the answer.

I never went back to escorting after that course I took.[†] And believe me, there were times when I was writing this play that I didn't know where my next meals were coming from. But somehow, they always came.

And though I'm far from perfect, I'm getting my integrity back. And I'm starting to take a good hard look at my addictions—all of them. *Ouch.* But my life is starting to work. And it makes me smile—really smile. And I wouldn't jeopardize that for all the *foie gras* in the world. I actually prefer cheese pizza to duck liver these days. And I like my Payless shoes. (Actually, these are Prada. But they're at least four seasons old!)

And yea, though I walk through the valley of the shadow of a narcissistic personality disorder—fear not! I've gone back to church a few times—especially at Christmas. I can't help it. I miss the music!

(*Mormon Tabernacle Choir sings "I Heard the Bells on Christmas Day".*)

I sneak in and sit in the back with my kids. We just watch and listen. I sing with the congregation, but it's kinda hard for me to blend!

(*Joins in singing. Choir fades as the last line is sung* a cappella.)

> *For hate is strong and mocks the song*
> *Of "peace on earth, good will to men."*

[†] *Steven stopped escorting Nov. 9, 2001.*

I'm often asked if I still believe Mormonism is "true." (*Pause*) I think it's as true as you need to make it. And what's funny is, remember that course I took? I had learned some of those same "enlightened" concepts when I was a little boy—at church! I have to admit that Mormons are right about at least one thing—"Men are that they might have joy." I take pride in my Mormon pioneer heritage. (After all, I am a Mormon American Princess.) So I guess it would be fair to say I'm now a humanist . . . with residual Christian tendencies. I believe in justice and mercy . . . and miracles.

Sometimes I think it's a miracle I'm still alive. But if I were to die tonight, and I got to say just a quick prayer before I did, my closing prayer would be the same one I offered a long time ago in Portugal. Except I'd change one word, "*Nosso Pai Celestial, sou grato por minha **vida**.*"

"Heavenly Father, thank you for my life."

(*Recording of child's voice from top of show is heard again.*)

Okay, everybody ready? It will begin now!

(*Blackout. "Mormon Boy" plays at curtain call.*)

"Mormon Boy"
Music and lyrics by Steven Fales

Mormon Boy, fight the fight.
Mormon Boy, choose the right.
Mormon Boy, touch the sky.
Mormon Boy, don't you cry.
Mormon Boy true as true.
Mormon Boy, when you're through—
Mormon Boy, you will see,
You can be truly free.

I've been watching you across the room
And I must say I'm impressed.
You've got 'em all enrolled with your charm and talk,
Like Steve Young or Donny Osmond at their best.

But before I go, could I have a word?
There's somethin' I'd like to do.
I've got some advice to give for free.
See, I was once a lot like you.

Mormon Boy, you've got it down.
Never let 'em see you frown.
Shinin' for the world to see.
That's the only way to be.
Mormon Boy can pass the test.
Always gotta be the best.
Standin' for all that's true.
Yeah, I was once a lot like you.

I say keep the smile. Keep the look.
That's not a crime at all.
You can keep your drive and attitude,
Keep your chin up and your head up tall.
Just remember when you've had enough
And you're finally feelin' blue,
You've got a friend. Knock on my door.
I will be here for you.
'Cause I was just like you.

Mormon Boy, I had it down.
Never let 'em see me frown.
Shined for all the world to see.
Was the only way to be.
Mormon Boy could pass the test.
Always had to be the best.
Stood there for all that's true.
Heck, I was just like you.

How did I fall? I'm not quite sure.
But one day she was gone.
And with her all my hopes and dreams,

Everything seemed so wrong.
The life I'd had was all a blur,
Like nothin' I'd ever known.
But in its place, though just a trace,
Was something to call my own.

Mormon Boy, fight the fight.
Mormon Boy, choose the right.
Mormon Boy, touch the sky.
Mormon Boy, don't you cry.
Mormon Boy true as true.
Mormon Boy, when you're through—
Mormon Boy you will see,
You can be truly free.

Mormon Boy, get it down.
Sometimes it's okay to frown.
Shine for all the world to see
If that's the way you wanna be.
Mormon Boy, pass that test
If you need to be the best.
I'll tell you one thing is true,
I will be here for you.
'Cause I was just like you.
Mormon Boy, you can, too.

"John, I'm a prostitute. I think I'm HIV . . . !"
(Coconut Grove Playhouse)

"No one wears black in Utah." *(Carol Rosegg)*

Epilogue

*My **father**, who* is one of the most devoted members of the Mormon Church I know, came to the opening night of the Off-Broadway run. He led the standing ovation. At the curtain call, I was able to acknowledge him from the stage and tell him what a truly generous man he was, and to express my love and gratitude for being such a great dad and extraordinary grandfather. Opening night was the antithesis of excommunication—it was homecoming.

My **mother** asked a few years ago that she not be as present in the play as I had wanted to make her originally. She came to the very first performance of the world premiere in Salt Lake City and has been cheering me on from afar.

My uncle **John**, who is mentioned briefly in the show and is my mother's youngest brother, came to opening night as well. He is six years older and is more like a brother to me than an uncle. When I was being excommunicated, he flew to Salt Lake City to be with me—the only family member to offer such support. He sat outside during my Church Court and spent the afternoon with me. It was one of the kindest things anyone has ever done for me and we are still very close.

My aunt **Linda** came to opening night as well to accompany my father (her brother). My aunt Linda is the most unconditionally loving Mormon (and human being) I have ever met. She was the one who made the recording of me singing as a little boy that opens and closes the show. She is like a second mother to me. There is no one who makes me laugh and feel more at ease than she.

Emily and I are currently in couples therapy working hard to continue to resolve many of our issues that stem from things beyond my homosexuality. We signed up for a lifetime of learning and are both still committed to truth-seeking. We are becoming the friends we were when we were first engaged. Emily lent her voice to the show in a sound cue where I harmonize to a lullaby to our son. She has seen all the versions of the show, from the first reading at the Sunstone Symposium in Salt Lake City, to the latest version. I have made changes to the show at her request. My only regret is that we were not able to have a third child, but we are both head-over-heels in love with the two children we do have. We have spent many family vacations and done many activities together with our non-traditional family—including Disneyland (where we went on our honeymoon)! Emily has been in a committed relationship with her very straight boyfriend for over four years and is no longer active in the Mormon Church.

The **dynamic course leader** saw me perform when I did the play as a benefit for the Point Foundation at Lincoln Center. I was so honored. I never could have written this play without the personal breakthroughs she helped me have while doing the Landmark Forum.

Carol Lynn Pearson made many helpful suggestions as I wrote the play. Her best advice came in challenging me to be as generous as I could to Mormonism. She asked specifically that I add the scene with her on the beach. She says she had red flags about my homosexuality the first time she spoke with me on the phone. I appreciate her many kindnesses to me. I commissioned her oil portrait from internationally acclaimed gay Mormon artist, Trevor Southey. I believe that is something Gerald Pearson would have wanted. I have named the portrait "Prophetess."

The **Lizard**. Imagine my surprise when the lights came up on my play one night Off-Broadway and there sat my first client in the front row, dressed in a silk kimono and accompanied by the escort/boyfriend I mention in my show. It was one of the most intense and honest performances of my life. The Lizard gave me flowers as he stood up during the ovation. I greeted them in the lobby after the show, thanking them for coming. In his broken English, the Lizard told me that he was very proud of me and that he was returning home to Osaka to start the first gay men's chorus there. He will also be reuniting with his children who he says he has still not come out to. My escort ex-boyfriend told me that I was magnificent onstage and that he would call me. He still hasn't.

I have had many other former **johns** surprise me by seeing the show, including a former UN ambassador. Many were and are gentleman—

and a few have remained friends. No former clients have contributed financially in any way to the development of my work. Most investors have come from straight friends across the country—including Salt Lake City.

The **dirty blond** and I have been friends now for a long time. He has come to see my show several times. We have never slept together.

It is amazing to me how many **missionaries** from my mission to Portugal have come out of the closet, including the one I mention in my play. Many are active in Affirmation (GLBT Mormons).

The **bishop** who helped excommunicate me continues to pop up in my life, most recently at the baptisms of my two children into the Mormon Church. After my daughter's baptism he stopped me and told me that he just wanted me to know "what a great dad" he thought I was. I told him that I appreciated all the things that he has done for my little family when I wasn't able to be there. We both had tears in our eyes.

The **LDS Church** continues its fight against homosexuality which it lists as an enemy next to feminism and secular humanism. They recently read over every pulpit in the church meetinghouse their stance against gay marriage and urged its membership to vote accordingly. The Mormon Church, however has made dramatic strides in the past toward human rights once laws have been changed. Back in 1890 they did away with polygamy so Utah could become a state. Then they allowed blacks to hold the priesthood in 1978, years after the Civil Rights Movement. I remain hopeful that the Mormon Church will continue to soften its position.

I am currently single, having had some very significant relationships with several boyfriends who have had a spiritual life. I split my time mainly between Salt Lake City and New York City, juggling my kids and my career. Sobriety has been a revelation. I am so grateful for my many friends, and the family members who have warmed to me, including my brother James and his wife Lyndi who came to opening night in New York. And I hope that one day, family members who still will have nothing to do with me will have a change of heart. I am in therapy with a terrific therapist and am busy working on new projects as I continue to perform my play across the country. The play has been an important part of my healing process. I will soon be able to let "Mormon Boy" go.

I often take my children to see live performances of the Mormon Tabernacle Choir at Temple Square. The Choir represents the very best of my people. I want my children to know where they come from. My children are the hope of the Mormon Church—if they choose to play a part. I don't believe in "church" anymore, but I will never give up on my people. Though I'm no longer a Latter-day Saint, something about me will always be Mormon.

An Afterword on the Creative Process

"It's as the old prostitute once said. It's not the work—it's the stairs."

—Elaine Stritch
Elaine Stritch at Liberty

People often ask me why I bothered to show up for my Church Court, "And miss the chance to do a one-man show?!" That certainly wasn't running through my head as I was being tried as a homosexual, but it started to germinate shortly after my excommunication. The whole process was so bizarre, surreal, and fantastical I thought *someone* ought to write a play about it! I soon realized that maybe I was the one to do it. I'd had very limited experience in writing—I was just an *actor*. But something inside me knew this tale needed to be told.

After my perfect Mormon world fell apart, I fled Utah and moved to New York. I kept telling everyone I was going to write a one-man show about my excommunication. I was met with cynicism by friends and colleagues: "Yeah, right, Steven. You and every other narcissistic actor in New York and L.A." As I told my story at cocktail parties in Manhattan, I found I could hold a room captivated by my story. If nothing else, I left the marriage with a good story.

I didn't know where to begin. I gathered it must start by putting pen to paper. I bought a spiral notebook and started jotting ideas and experiences down. I started journaling my thoughts and experiences in notebooks, on index cards, on scratch pieces of paper—trying to capture images and words and important plot points as they would come, wherever I might be—at the gym, at work, in the park, in the shower, on a plane or subway. Ultimately all these bits and pieces would be put in a pile on my table and story-boarded across my living room. It was a very messy and intuitive creative process with more rhyme than reason.

I must also give credit to my former mother-in-law for inspiring me to write. I'd seen Carol Lynn Pearson put her passion to work and produce her educational one-woman play, *Mother Wove the Morning*, all across the country and internationally, so I had some pretty good mapping on how to do it. I'd now just plug myself into her formula. I also began seeing and reading the work of as many solo artists as I could: Tim Miller, Margaret Cho, John Leguizamo, Eric Bogosian, David Drake, Lily Tomlin, Elaine Stritch, just to name a few. But nothing inspired me like my mother-in-law's work—nothing.

After six months of getting sidetracked in a whirlwind of gay adolescent hedonism and debauchery, which included escorting (which I never intended to divulge!) and spinning my wheels at soap opera auditions (I think they could tell I was wearing a hairpiece!), I decided to go for it.

I work best under pressure and when there's everything at stake. I decided that I needed some deadlines: a date for a reading and a date for an opening. I knew I wanted to premiere the show in Salt Lake City. I figured if I could make it there, I could make it anywhere! When I first booked the black box theatre in downtown Salt Lake City for the world premiere, I still hadn't written it. I booked it on pure faith. Luckily they held the dates without a deposit until I could borrow enough money from some straight Mormon friends in Salt Lake whose son had just come out. I knew I had something to say; I now had six months to figure out how to say it.

Now I just needed an official staged reading. I decided to ask Dan Wootherspoon, the editor of *Sunstone Magazine* if I could do a reading at the Sunstone Symposium in August 2001 in Salt Lake City. I decided I wanted the Sunstone audience to guide my tone: Mormons who are smart yet true of heart, a bit irreverent but respectful, goodwill, and no swearing or nudity. Sunstone is a controversial organization that is a forum for Mormon intellectual thought and art. It's like the Mormon Fringe Festival. The Brethren do not approve of its existence. It is considered apostate. This was an opportunity to see what sympathetic members of the church would think of my story. I had a built-in audience since Carol Lynn Pearson was a favorite speaker and practically Sunstone's cover girl, having written controversial articles in the past like "Could Feminism Have Saved the Nephites [in The Book of Mormon?]". Sunstone enthusiastically accepted my proposal. I was now all set to dig into my own writing.

I made a deliberate choice to stop auditioning for anything else. I cut out all distractions and banished myself to my laptop to meet my self-inflicted deadline.

It hadn't even been a year since my divorce and excommunication, but I knew if I didn't freeze-dry my emotions and the sordid details in ink while they were fresh, I might lose them forever. I didn't want to lose my edge or my passion. Then what would I have to contribute to the Cause? (Looking back, I'm glad I wrote it when I did. Sometimes I ask myself, "Did that really happen like that? Did I really feel that way?")

When Carol Lynn Pearson realized that I was dead set on writing my show, she gave me some excellent advice—which I took to heart. She said, "Now, we want to like you. If you get up onstage and rant and are angry, we are not going to like you."

And I wanted to be honest, but also fair. And that meant I needed to be generous, even when I didn't feel like it. There was plenty to rip on—especially doctrine. I didn't need to rip on everything. I could hold the Church accountable for its institutionalized bigotry and give credit to the goodness of the people and the culture.

I agreed with Carol Lynn that the play shouldn't be another self-indulgent whiny gay victim play—and I didn't want it to come across too serious, or cheesy/sentimental, or significant. And I didn't want it to be another gay romp with nudity. I wanted my play to be truthful, respectful, fair, generous of spirit, but above all, funny. So *Confessions of a Mormon Boy* began as a stand-up comedy routine.

I decided to take a stand-up class from the American Comedy Institute in New York led by Stephen Rosenfield. Stand-up had been calling to me throughout the years, but it terrified me. I had done a brief assignment in stand-up in graduate school that wasn't too encouraging. Besides, I thought of myself as an inhibited, over-articulating, "classically" trained musical theatre actor with a masters degree from a "wannabe Yale School of Drama" to prove it. I didn't have a clue how to get up in front of a room and be myself and be funny. Sometimes it's still a challenge. Give me a script to play anyone else—just don't make me play myself. But I figured if I was now free to be me—and if humor came from a wellspring of pain, I had plenty of comic fodder and tons of emotional baggage to draw from.

The workshop was a revelation. I found I couldn't wait to get up in front of a room full of other humans, be myself (whoever that was), and just talk about the absurdities of life. I was starving for this kind of communing with an audience. It excited and satisfied and terrified me in a way that doing straight plays and musicals had never done before. The class changed my life. I took it twice. People actually laughed. I was told I had potential.

Each class culminated in a group performance at Caroline's on Broadway, Stand-Up New York, or Don't Tell Mama. We each had five minutes. My first round was at Caroline's. The shows were at obscure, non-prime-time slots made up of short five-minute sets—two-drink minimum. Our audiences were mainly made up of family and friends, no outside advertising. There was so much goodwill. I felt safe and accepted. I had come home and joined the human race. The club was like being at a non-traditional family night. My set always started out, "Hi, I'm Steven Fales. And I'm a Mormon. And that's why I smile like this!" I had found my persona and my comic voice.

What my ex-wife will confirm is that if I write an idea down, sooner or later it comes to pass. I came up with a title for my show wrote it on a yellow Post-it and stuck it on my bathroom mirror:

CONFESSIONS OF A MORMON BOY
Eagle Scout
Missionary
Husband
Father
Homosexual ...
Human

The process of writing the first draft of the show involved days and weeks over several months literally pouring my soul into my laptop.

Bills laid unpaid from practically no income (I wasn't escorting any-more—but had gotten a grant from an old client and a few former professors from graduate school and my uncle John helped me sur-vive), dishes were piling up in the sink, and eating peanut butter and jelly sandwiches to survive—sweltering in the muggy summer heat with the windows open in my huge, crazy, eclectic, prewar fifth-story " Rose-mary's Baby" corner Upper West Side apartment that I subletted from an equally eccentric theatre impresario from South Africa.

As I wrote, I was frequently reduced to tears from crying so hard or laughing so hysterically. People often say, "It must be so cathartic reliv-ing your life night after night onstage." What is truly cathartic is the writing! Especially when you write from your guts and liver. I actually felt divine guidance and reassurance as I wrote in this almost Diony-sian frenzy. I couldn't believe what would pour out. It was as if the text itself was meant to be written. Tangent led to tangent. Though I knew I couldn't use a lot of it, my confidence grew as a writer. I tried not to edit myself as draft after draft started writing itself. I couldn't keep my mind still or type fast enough for all the ideas that were popping.

I pored over old journals and letters. Listened to old recordings and video tapes. Examined every aspect of my life from a theatrical point of view. I rarely took time to sleep or eat. My one occasional time-out indulgence was throwing "to go" sushi in my backpack and roller-blading with my shirt off (and in short shorts), racing toward the Twin Towers from Riverside Park along the Hudson River to read through my latest draft in Battery Park City—whilst casually cruisin' the other shirt-less men. The mighty Twin Towers that were my friends and compass would be gone within a few weeks of those excursions.

I was sober when I wrote.

Once I finally got a draft together, I had a reading in my apartment for friends and colleagues, cramming thirty people in my living room, holding them hostage for over two hours with no bathroom break and no way to slip out the back unnoticed! The feedback was genuinely encouraging with people often moved to tears. They would tell me that time seemed to fly by.

I was still very nervous to do the Sunstone reading because my ex-wife, Emily, accepted my invitation to come. After the reading, she ran up to the stage and gave me an embrace that meant the world to me. She had tears in her eyes. She told me it was brilliant as she flung her arms around me. I felt if I could get that kind of response from Emily (in addition to the standing ovation), I knew I must be on the right track. Even if it was the fast track to hell! Sunstone sold the audio tape recording of the session like hotcakes.

I returned to New York in time for 9/11. All my legit jobs dried up, so I had lots of time to do rewrites. I had another reading in my apartment. Then I returned for another visit to see my kids in Salt Lake City in early October. This time the reading was at the Spauldings' ("that cool non-LDS family with three kids—Democrats"). It went very well. I then went back to New York to deal with the continued chaos there.

Just four weeks before I was to open in Salt Lake City, I lost my Juilliard-trained director and his boyfriend designer. They were both based in Salt Lake and New York and we had worked out what I thought was a great financial deal. They called up with no warning and no explanation and dumped the project. I felt so betrayed. I couldn't believe they could just break their commitment like that. I thought we were working so well together. I was left alone to pull it off. I picked up the promotional pieces and took the helm of all duties and began to panic. I was faced with being the writer, actor, costume, set and lighting designer, press agent, the producer, fundraiser, and now the director! It was totally insane and I was completely overwhelmed. But the theatre was booked. The postcards were printed. I had to go through with it.

When this all blew up, I had been writing a section about Heavenly Mother in the show and so she had been on my mind quite a lot. I was developing her into a major character in the original Utah version. (Heavenly Mother is the token female deity in Mormonism.) Later that day after I was passing by St. Patrick's Cathedral, I felt prompted to go in. The whole "Catholic thing" was so foreign to my Mormon sensibilities, but I found my way to the Virgin Mary shrine. I used one of my last remaining dollars to buy one of those little white votive candles (I couldn't steal from the Church!). As I lit it, I said a fervent little prayer: "Heavenly Mother, I need your help. I can't do this alone. It's just too much. It's just too big. If this is to be a success and is meant to be, please take care of the details."

About two weeks before I was to fly to Salt Lake to do the show (by now the press releases were sent and I'd already been doing phone interviews with Salt Lake City papers), I did something that seemed totally ridiculous at the time. I took a weekend off to do a course called the Landmark Forum. I seriously didn't have time to do it, but my extraordinary friends, the Spauldings—had been so convincing about the benefits, I couldn't let them down. Or pass up the scholarship. I went. That is the course I took that I mention in my show. The Landmark Forum changed my life and started me on a path of transformation. I finished the course resolving to never go back to escorting and was filled with excitement to pull off the impossible in Salt Lake City.

I arrived via JetBlue on a Sunday in late November and worked all week on the show to get it up for the Friday preview, the day after Thanksgiving. I was still trying to memorize the piece as I shopped for props and led the design and tech team.

I'd been working at a fever pitch all week buying props, building scenery, fixing my costume, making the star drop with thread and balled up tin foil, focusing lights, writing programs, running to Kinko's, cutting out whole paragraphs of the script at the last minute, re-thinking acting transitions, changing choreography, re-blocking my half-baked staging, putting out the 101 fires that flare up before you give birth to your drama love child. If grad school taught me anything it was how to move heaven and earth to mount a show and do a million things at once. But the Landmark Forum gave me a peace and serenity. I floated along as if I were in the eye of the storm. I seemed to be unstoppable.

Thanksgiving was on a Thursday and I took the day off to memorize my lines since the theatre was locked up. On Friday, the day of the first paid public preview, I was up at five that morning singing my "You and Utah" song on a "Good Morning Utah" TV program. But that afternoon I was exhausted and getting sick. We were in the middle of our tech/dress rehearsal when I couldn't remember half my lines and was losing my voice. I couldn't concentrate—my body mic kept falling off. And half the light and sound cues were late or wrong! At around 4:00 P.M. I stopped mid-rehearsal and told everyone to just finish doing whatever they could without me and I would be back for my call time at 6:00 P.M.

The show would still go on at 8:00 P.M. It had to. But I honestly didn't know how I would get through it.

I needed to get something to eat and just *be still*. It was cold outside and you could smell snow was on its way. I went to P. F. Chang's next door but it was way too noisy. I needed quiet. I crossed the street to a posh gourmet restaurant.

I rapped on the door. It wasn't yet open for dinner, but the bartender let me in anyway. I sat at a table by the bar and told him I desperately needed a cup of hot tea for my throat. I then called my friend Sharon Spaulding on my cell phone. (She's the one who got me to take the Forum. The one whose family took me in temporarily after my divorce and excommunication. I knew their basement better than they for all the time I'd spent staying with them.) She answered and I burst into tears of despair.

What was I doing? This was all a huge mistake. I was going to fail. Right there in front of everyone—including Emily. Right there in SALT LAKE CITY! Just a few blocks away from the Mormon Vatican. Would my kids curse my name forever for what I was about to do? How much more scrutiny was I setting myself up for? And what would happen when the conservative world someday found out that this poor excommunicated boy had been a hooker just a few weeks before? (Note that the first version of my show did not deal with escorting or crystal meth!) What kind of credibility would my "affecting" play have then?! Did I really think I could take the homosexual shame of their grandfather Gerald and now their own father and make some kind of lemonade out of this mess? Was this really for my kids—or for me? Who was I kidding? Wasn't I really out to punish Emily for divorcing me and the Church for excommunicating me? What kind of a twisted, Freudian, narcissistic "valentine" was this?! I just sobbed and sobbed.

After listening to me blubber on and on, Sharon lovingly and firmly said, "Okay, Steven. You've done lots of stupid things in your life. But what is it that you want to do *now*?" And the answer came immediately as I heaved one last giant sob. The answer came out so strong and spontaneous that I was surprised to hear myself say, "All I want to do is spin as much love on that stage that it transforms everyone who sees it!" And instantly my fear was gone, and I stopped crying. There was silence on the other end. "Then that's what you are going to do," she said matter-of-factly.

I had never felt more clarity or more sense of purpose. With white-hot lucidity, I felt no matter what happened, my play was based in love (and truth!). It was not possible to fail. "Charity never Fales!"

Sharon Spaulding. My Catholic angel. She was going to be coming that night with her husband Carl and all their close friends, which felt so great. I needed all the support I could get.

The restaurant was very expensive. But I needed a really good meal. The kitchen finally opened and the staff set up a table for me near the fireplace in the back. They had all seen me crying and were trying to help as much as they could—figuring out I was about to do the show across the street. I had a fifty-dollar bill given to me by a senior technician at the theatre who believed in my work and the message. That was all the money I had until the box office receipts trickled in—if any. The meal cost about $40. I had just enough for a tip and to put more money in my parking meter for the car I was borrowing from another friend. The service was truly the best I'd ever experienced—even in New York. I needed a little TLC—and quiet—as I savored the seared rare ahi tuna before the dinner crowd converged on the restaurant.

I walked out a new man. My voice and energy were coming back. I couldn't wait to get on that stage. It didn't matter if I forgot my lines. I was going to take the audience and stage by storm.

I walked across the street to check in with the box office before the show. *They told me the preview was sold-out.* Mostly filled with friends and well-wishers from Affirmation—the local gay and lesbian Mormons. All the free press and stories in the local liberal papers was worth its weight in gold—since I had no real advertising budget to speak of.

I could feel the energy of the audience from my dressing room speaker. I could hear the pre-show music "My Turn on Earth". It was packed to overflowing.

Sharon and her husband and all their friends were not able to get tickets. They came too late! They didn't think to buy advanced tickets for a preview, and I had been too scattered to put comps aside. I got their note just before I went on stage congratulating me on my sell-out and that they would come again soon.

I could feel the expectation of the counter-culture crowd of Salt Lake pressing in. "Another world premiere?" Would it be another waste of time (and $15) watching another flailing, eager LDS artist attempting his fifteen minutes of Wasatch Front fame?

The lights went out. My flashlight went on. The star-drop illuminated. And I pulled-my own curtain as I walked out on stage in the dark of my "somewhere in eternity" set. I met their energy, absorbing it, regenerating it, and sending it back with the force of hydroelectric turbine generators at Hoover Dam. But I felt an inner peace. I felt in control—it all went so smoothly. I remembered all my lines. The body mic stayed on. The sound and light cues were right on. (God bless my stage manager who ran the light and sound board!) My comic timing was right on, uncertain blocking became spontaneously certain. I gave a performance I will personally never forget and for which I will be forever grateful. It flowed—words, inflection, emotion, gesture, dance. I could feel the audience with me every step of the way. The laughter! The sobs! The moments of dead silence . . . it was landing just as I'd hoped.

At the curtain call, I was blown away by the thunderous applause and standing ovation. After the performance, I met Emily. She told me that I left the marriage with the Pearson family wit. It was the best compliment I have ever received.

After the show, I changed out of costume and drove home alone in the snow.

The run sold out. I added an extra performance to accommodate the demand. I knew I was on to something. The run exceeded all my expectations. Audiences were touched, reviews were glowing, emails of gratitude poured in, and I made more money in those two weeks than I had before in my life (which I blew on Emily and my kids for Christmas that year in New York City!). As they say in show-biz, "You can't make a living. But you can sure make a killing!"

And as you can also see, my dream of having my show play Off-Broadway eventually came to pass. "Thank you, Heavenly Mother!"

PART TWO

Bonus Features

"Excuse me, St. Peter? Is Heavenly Mother there? I'd like to talk to Heavenly Mother."

(Courtesy of Keith Jochim)

Excerpt from the Original Utah Script

Here is an excerpt from the original Utah version of *Confessions of a Mormon Boy*, which started as a reading at the 2001 Salt Lake Sunstone Symposium and had its world premiere at the Rose Wagner Performing Arts Center in Salt Lake City, November 23, 2001. The two-week run sold out, and an additional performance was added to accommodate the demand. The play has obviously undergone significant rewrites. Much of the original Utah/Mormon in-humor has been taken out in the new "gentile" version (including the Pre-existence, Heavenly Mother and the theatrical convention of using St. Peter). This version of the play was published in its entirety with production photos in the December 2003 issue of *Sunstone* magazine. The church-owned *Deseret News* has still never reviewed my play.

∽

(A backdrop of stars somewhere in eternity. A flashlight appears. A voice is heard in the dark.)

Excuse me, St. Peter? Is Heavenly Mother there? I'd like to talk to Heavenly Mother. Could you please tell her I'm here? You don't know who that is? Look pal, I know you're the only one up here that's not a Mormon, but you really should know who your Heavenly Mother is—the *wife* of Heavenly Father. Could you please turn on some lights? I know I'm in Outer Darkness, but this is ridiculous!

(*Blinding floodlights come up revealing Steven in a white penitentiary jumpsuit with black "jailbird" stripes and a huge pink triangle on the back. He is holding a backpack filled with personal props, a bouquet of daffodils, and, of course, the flashlight. The stage looks like an opening night party for a new nightclub or Broadway musical. There is a red carpet downstage roped of with white velvet ropes and stanchions, ficus trees with white lights, a cocktail table with a white satin tablecloth, fresh white roses, and votive candles. There is a disco ball hanging and a white poster that reads in large gold letters:* CELESTIAL KINGDOM–SOME VISITORS WELCOME. *Steven continues to address St. Peter.*)

Thank you! Heavenly Mother said she would put my name on the list for her Celestial Tea Party, just in case the Judgment didn't go well for me. It obviously didn't. Am I on it? Brother Fales, Steven H. I'm not? Oh, she must have forgotten. It's an easy mistake. I'm sure it's okay. Yes, I know homosexuals aren't allowed to go to heaven, but this is an exception. I have permission from the glorified, resurrected Diva herself. She invited me personally. I promise I'll leave just as soon as it's over. Now don't tell me it's not going on. I saw the flyers down in Hell. I know it's today. And my kids are in there. So I'm coming in!

(*Steven steps on the red carpet and burns his feet. Sirens go off.*)

Ouch! Hot! Hot! Hot! Hot! Hot! Good grief!
Look, I came all the way from the Telestial Kingdom to be here. I had to sneak past security. Then I rode a million light years up the escalator through the Terrestrial Kingdom where I finally found the glass elevator to the Celestial Kingdom. Oh, St. Peter, don't tell me you don't know about Mormon Eternity!

(*Steven turns over the poster and draws the Plan of Salvation with bionic speed.*)

The Celestial Kingdom, Heaven, where you're here standing, guarding these Pearly Gates? That's only for the really good Mormons. (How did you get here? Even the popes live down with me.) The Terrestrial kingdom is where the okay Mormons go. And the Telestial Kingdom, hell, is where the really bad Mormons (and everyone else) go.

Heavenly Mother told me in the Pre-existence that I was invited to her Celestial Tea Party. The *Pre-existence* Oh, you Catholics don't know *anything*! The Pre-existence is where we lived with Heavenly Father and Mother before we came to Earth. You know, where everyone was Mormon. We all smiled like this. (*Steven flashes his "Mormon" smile.*) It was the coolest place. Kinda like Krypton, where Superman lived before he came to Earth in that egg-ship. Everything was in its perfectly created pre-mortal form, and everyone was friendly and happy because nothing bad had ever happened to anyone. And just like Superman had to watch all those videos about trees and Shakespeare and stuff, we had classes to learn about mortality while we anxiously waited to go down to Earth, where we would gain a body and suffer. Except when we got there, we would forget it all. Except for me. I remember *everything*.

I remember I was in love with Jimmy Flinders. The first time I saw him was at a class we were taking on dating and eternal marriage. I was there with my best friend, Emily. We were learning how to get a husband down on Earth. We were chatting away like we always did, when Jimmy walked in the Pre-mortal Conference Center. Talk about a First Vision. He was blond, blue-eyed, 185 pounds, six feet tall—tanned, toned, tight muscular swimmer's build. There was no question he was the tops! I wanted so bad to be his husband . . . his wife . . . his eternal companion! (After we finished our two-year missions on Earth, of course, and our degrees in musical theatre at Brigham Young University. You know, "the Lord's University"?) Emily and I were fighting over him:

"He's mine!"

"No, he's mine!"

"He's looking at me!"

"He saw me first!"

After the closing prayer, we jumped out of our seats and raced towards Jimmy. I was afraid Emily would get there before me. I could never compete with her. She was blonde and absolutely gorgeous, not to mention the nicest and funniest girl in the Pre-existence. If she talked to him first, I would lose my chance. I was in the lead, but as I rounded the refreshment table, the director of the Pre-mortal Mormon Tabernacle Choir, Brother Lockhart, stepped in front of me. I crashed into the punch bowl. Red punch and Oreos went flying everywhere. Sure enough, Emily got a date with Jimmy to the Pre-mortal Gold and Green Ball. All I got was a mop and a seat in the alto section in the choir.

Do you have time for this, St. Peter? Good. Time doesn't exist here anyway, you know.

The Pre-mortal premiere of the long-running, smash hit, Mormon mega-musical *Saturdays' Warrior* had just ended. Jimmy had made quite a name for himself as a leading man in that production. I was a dancer in the chorus. But I didn't mind the chorus, as long as I could watch Jimmy from the wings as he gave them his big solo number in the second act. *"I'll wait for you, Jimmy!"*

Now auditions were being held for the revival of my favorite Mormon musical, *My Turn on Earth*. It was clear that Jimmy was going to play the male lead—again! You know, the Jesus part who then gets to play the husband part who marries the female lead, Barbara? Brother Stanislav-sky said Jimmy naturally acted the part better. Whatever! Jimmy didn't even like acting or the theatre. He just stood there and acted all butch so everyone would fall in love with him. That's not acting. Me playing butch—now *that* would be acting!

So I decided I wanted to play the Barbara part. Not only would I be playing a leading part worthy of my talent, but on stage I would get to marry Jimmy. At the audition, I just kept thinking of him:

(*Sings from* The King and I)

> *In these dreams I've loved you so*
> *That by now I think I know*
> *What it's like to be loved by you.*
> *I will—*

"Next!"

Can you believe they cut me off? I didn't even get to sing my high note, for Pete's sake! (Oh, sorry. I didn't mean to take your name in vain.) So guess who got the part? Emily. Again! I mean, just because her future mother would write the show was no excuse. I could belt higher than any of the other girls, and I had the best split leaps in my primordial dispensation—not to mention they should always give the role to the best actress!

Well, I did get cast. You know the part I got? Satan. He doesn't get to marry anyone! Now I would never get to marry Jimmy! So you want to know what I did? I learned the entire Barbara part behind Emily's back just in case she got her orders to go to Earth in the middle of a performance. Someone would have to fill in, and I would be ready! (*Sings*) *"Emily, time to go home!"*

Getting sent to Earth at a moment's notice was always a possibility. Once, during a particularly long candy-wrapper matinee, we were all on stage singing: *"The world turns 'round like a merry-go-round. It lets some off, and it takes some on."* There we were: Jimmy, Emily, Dave, Marci, and me. And right in the middle of the number, Marci starts floating up out of theatre and down towards Earth with a look of utter surprise on her face. (*Sings*) *"It ends with death. It begins with birth. And it's my turn—*Good-bye, Marci! (Good-bye, bass section.)." Then, as Dave and I are doing the dance lift Marci and I usually do, he starts to go, too. But he's determined to finish the number. So, he's clinging to me, clawing at the scenery, grabbing whatever he can to stay on stage—chairs, a table. "Have a nice life, Dave! (*Sings*) *It's your turn on Earth.*" (Minutes later a pregnant woman in a remote village in Madagascar gave birth to a boy and two chairs. Now that's the magic of live theatre!)

I knew Dave wasn't a good performer because only the really bad ones (and lemurs) go to Madagascar. If you didn't want to end up there—or another non-elect country—you knew you had to razzle-dazzle 'em. There was no way I was going somewhere non-elect. I was going to Broadway! That's why I made sure my Satan was especially wicked every time. Like in the War-in-Heaven scene, where Jesus and I battle over whose plan everyone should follow down on Earth.

(*Sings in a sexy, exaggerated style*)

> *I have a plan.*
> *It will save every man.*
> *I will force them to live righteously.*
> *They won't have to choose—*

> *Not one we will lose—*
> *And give all the glory to me.*
> *Give it to me!*

Of course, Jesus always won that scene in the show. But since Jimmy was so cute playing Jesus, I didn't mind a bit.

∾

One day after rehearsal, I ran into Jimmy who was practicing the love duet he sings with Barbara, "Eternity Is You." He was having difficulty with the harmony.

"Want some help?"

"Sure. Thanks, dude."

(*Sings*) "*Looking at you, I can see right through to eternity.*"

We blended so well together. And as I looked into his eyes "*Eternity is you*," I could swear I saw eternity. So I kissed him. Hard. He was surprised. I could tell. He decked me. I went flying across the rehearsal cloud.

"Well, someone had to do it. And it wouldn't be right if it was Heavenly Father!"

I begged him, "Please don't turn me in to Heavenly Father!"

He didn't. He turned me in to Heavenly Mother.

I was summoned to the Pre-mortal Lion House. Heavenly Mother was holding high tea in the Celestial Tea Room (where they serve that delicious non-caffeine Celestial Seasonings chamomile tea). She was finishing her weekly support group for all the women who would be polygamist wives. It was getting really heated in there, so I just waited in the lobby where I watched *Who Wants to Be a Mormon Millionaire?* Until the sisters finally came out. There was Emma Smith:

"Hi, Emma!" (Boy, did she look pissed.)

I was a little nervous. It was so rare to actually see Heavenly Mother I forgot what she looked like. She came sweeping into the room. "Is that my little Steven? Welcome back, *dahling*!" Now I knew why they never talked about her. She's fabulous! She was Auntie Mame, Betty Davis, Martha Stewart, and Oprah Winfrey all rolled into one.

We immediately hit it off. I complimented her ZCMI tea set and offered a few decorating tips as I rearranged the flowers on the table.

Then I helped her pick out her veil for the Pre-ordination High Priest Gala to be held later that evening. She said, "Why do I always have to sit in the back and wear a veil? I am the mother of all Creation, dagnab it! Where are we, Pre-mortal Afghanistan?" She was also upset she didn't have her own email address on the Celestial Internet. She laughed as she told me that she'd secretly gotten hold of Heavenly Father's password. "Just four simple letters. Now I can send inspiration to my children whenever the heck I like!" We spent the rest of the time swapping Jell-O recipes and reciting our favorite Carol Lynn Pearson poetry: "Today you came running, with a small specked egg warm in your hand . . . "

Before we knew it, it was time for her to go. I think she forgot why I'd been summoned to meet her. I rushed to help her put on her veil, her gloves, and her black mink stole. "Thank you, my dahling boy. (*Pause*) Steven, is there anything special you'd like down on Earth? Anything at all! A share at Fire Island or a Prada gift certificate, perhaps?"

"I just want to marry Jimmy Flinders."

"Yes, he is a stud, isn't he? Well, don't tell your Heavenly Father, but I'll see what I can do. You must join me and the entire Relief Society for my Celestial Tea Party when everything is all said and done. You'll fit right in. Oh! If the Judgment doesn't go well for you, I'll leave your name at the Pearly Gates. (Would you be a dear and light this for me? Thank you, dahling. Can you believe it? I'm as old as time, and I'm still sneaking cigarettes!) Just tell St. Peter you're here, and I'll have him buzz you right in!"

⁓

I am telling the truth, St. Peter. You think I just made all this up? Could you please check the list again? Brother Fales. "F" as in Frank. Not F-A-I-L-S. *F-A-L-E-S.* Fales is an old Welsh name meaning "son of Fagel." Fagel is spelled F-A-G-e-l. Fagel, sometimes pronounced *feyghella*, also means "to be glad," which is a synonym for *happy* or *gay*—and that's why I smile like this. (*Smiles*) So am I on the list? Steve Young, Donny Osmond, Orrin Hatch . . . That's the Terrestrial list. I'm on the *Te*lestial list. Well, tell them to find it and fax it up! Please! (*Sighs*)

I can't wait to see my kids again. It feels like twenty millennia have passed. But who's counting? Judgment Day was the last time I saw them. What a fiasco! My attorney was late, and my star witness testified against me—bitter old queen! I was screaming bloody murder when they tore me away from my kids. They sentenced me to eternal damnation with no visitation rights until the end of eternity! They let me keep this picture of them though. (*Pulls frame out of backpack and shows to St. Peter*) I keep it by my cot in my studio apartment on the Lower East Side of Hell. Here's my son and daughter when they were five and three. Just before the divorce. See the light in their eyes?

I tried to be a good father. We'd wrestle, put puzzles together, jump on the trampoline. I'd read them *Harry Potter* books. I even taught them Shakespeare monologues when they could barely even speak. I know my son would have preferred to go to a Yankees game instead of the Metropolitan Museum of Art when they came to visit me in New York, but that Jacqueline Kennedy exhibit was not to be missed! I took them to their first Broadway show, *The Lion King*. I was Mufasa. They were my Simba and Nala. Our favorite thing to do was to put on the ABBA CDs and dance around the living room. (*Sings*) *"Angel Eyes, one look and you're hypnotized . . ."* We'd fly and fly and fly. Oh, I can't *wait* to see them!

Now where was I? The Pre-existence! So anyway, I left the Celestial Tea Room so excited. The first thing I wanted to do was find Emily and tell her what Heavenly Mother had said about Jimmy and me. I thought I'd cut across Pre-mortal Temple Square. The trees were all lit up. (They keep it Christmas all year 'round so they don't have to take the lights down.) Everything was still. A hazy white mist descended and hovered over the ground like the Holy Ghost. I could hear crying. I followed the sound toward the temple. As I got closer I could make out the figure of a little girl who was sobbing on the steps. No one is supposed to cry in the Pre-existence! I put my hand on her shoulder. She looked up at me with the most beautiful brown eyes:

"What's wrong?"

She just handed me her golden envelope. That's the envelope your orders to go to Earth come in. It's where you learn all the horrible things that are going to happen to you. It's like a patriarchal blessing *before* you go to Earth. You're not supposed to be sad or question your assignment or where you are sent because we are told that everyone will suffer. Can you believe I still have it?

(*Reads*)

Dear Sister Nine Hundred Sixty-seven Billion, One Hundred Thousand and Three:

Having been true and faithful in many things, we desire to give unto you your orders to go unto Earth. You will be one of ten children who will have the gospel literally beat into you by your parents in Reno, Nevada. Without knowing how to balance a checkbook, you will be married off before your high school graduation. Everyone will expect perfection from you as you raise six children. Don't expect much help from your husband. He will be busy going to medical school, delivering babies, fulfilling church callings, caring for his horses, and doing genealogy in all his spare time. After your divorce, with no degree or skills, your health failing, and an abusive second marriage, you will fight depression, want to die most of the time, and be thought of by everyone as crazy. You're a real trooper, Sister.

'Preciate ya!
Your Heavenly Father (and Uncles).

I said, "That's pretty bad. It must really suck to be a girl. I'm glad I'm not one. (I only act like one.) But, hey! I can go down and help you through the hard times. I love to cook, clean, and sew. I'm great at curling bangs and changing diapers. When you're pregnant, I'll bring you pans to throw up in so you won't have to crawl to the toilet. I'll be there for you when your husbands are not, and I'll treat you the way you deserve to be treated. Let's hang out. It'll be fun!"

So she agreed to be my mother, and we filled out the paper work. As soon as she signed her name, she floated up past the illuminated spires of the temple and out of sight.

I thought, "This is great!" Not only did I know who my husband was going to be, I knew who my mother was! I couldn't wait to tell Emily. But when I found her on the Pre-mortal BYU campus, I could tell something was really troubling her. She had just gotten her orders! She told me that her father, whom she would love more than anyone in the world, would die of a disease called AIDS when she was only sixteen. This would send her into years of depression. To top it off, she would have this terrible condition that would make her want to win an Academy Award, which would take her to Hollywood where her butt would be on *Baywatch*. Then she would escape to Salt Lake City and fall in love with the man of her dreams. But after a short time, he would die in her arms of cancer. But the very next day she would meet her first husband. He would be a very cute boy who liked ABBA songs and who reminded her a whole lot of her father. Especially the part about being gay. (I thought, "Cool! What a cool thing to marry someone happy!") They would have two incredible children and together they would endure poverty and graduate school in the backwoods of Connecticut (where the ward was nothing like the wards in Utah). Then after being married almost seven years, they would both stop smiling because—

Just then, a messenger handed me a golden envelope. *My* orders! I was so excited I ripped it open:

(*Reads*)

Brother Fales:
Having been true and faithful in many things, we desire to give unto you your orders to go unto Earth. You will be gay. Good luck!

Gay? Cool! But why do you need good luck if you're going to be happy? Didn't Emily's orders say something about happy, too? Her gay father? And the father of her children? I liked ABBA songs. What if I was to be Emily's "happy" husband? (*Pause.*) Yuck! We were far too good of friends to let *that* happen! Besides, I already knew who I was going to marry. Heavenly Mother said!

Emily went back to reading me her orders: "Then after being married for almost seven years, you will both stop smiling because—

"Jimmy!"

There he was coming out of the Pre-mortal Marriott Center.

"Jimmy, wait up! You'll be all right, Em. We all will. I just know it. I've gotta run. You're my best friend, Em. I'll see you when we get back from Earth. Can't wait to see your fabulous butt on *Baywatch!* Look for me, Em. I'll be the happy one with good luck—on Broadway! Hey, Jimmy! *Dude!* Wait up!"

I didn't even reach Jimmy before I started to float away into the starry black sky toward Earth. Down, down I floated, across the Atlantic. There was Broadway! Yes! But, no. I kept floating west over the Rocky Mountains, where I landed in Utah County Hospital in Provo, Utah. The last thing I remember, I was looking around for Jimmy. Where was he?

Am I boring you, St. Peter? Well, you were yawning . . .

(Steven continues to tell St. Peter his story of life down on earth as a gay Mormon. Much of the story is similarly related in the "gentile" version that has been done in New York and across the country. At one point in the story St. Peter interrupts.)

What did you say, St. Peter? The list came in! Finally! Oh, boy, the lucky ones from Hell who get to go to the party: Sonja Johnson (Isn't she still fighting for ERA? They let her in?), Emma Smith (Brigham Young said she was going to Hell in a hand basket), Elton John! I guess Princess Di arranged for him to play. You know, she was baptized for the dead in the temple after she was killed—so she's Mormon now. You see, if you're not a Mormon when you die, you go straight to Spirit Prison—kinda like purgatory. There you wait to be baptized by proxy in a big baptismal font in a temple down on Earth. If you accept that baptism, it's like a Get-Out-Of-Jail-Free card. You can bet that anyone famous, the Church did their work for them. Elvis, Judy Garland, and all the signers of the Declaration of Independence—

I'm not on the list?! HEAVENLY MOTHER!! Don't you shush me! I'm telling you, I was invited. Would you please send some cherubim, seraphim, or sing-an-hymn and just tell her I'm here. Thank you! I know we're here for eternity, but does *this* have to take that long?

You want to hear about my Church Court? Well, I'll tell you anyway . . .

(Steven continues to tell his story.)

They're back? What do you mean they can't find her? How hard can it be to find the Queen Bee herself? Do you mind if I try? (*Steps on red carpet*) *Ouch! Hot! Hot! Hot! Hot! Hot!*

I know! My kids! Go tell my kids I'm here. They can go find Heavenly Mother for me. My son is tall, blonde, smart. My daughter is gorgeous, dark hair, clever. They're both witty and talented and have my brown eyes. Please hurry. I really don't have all eternity.

(*After buying more time, waiting and waiting unsuccessfully to find out if his name is on the list, Steven's children show up at the end of the play to help. Steven's story has moved St. Peter to tears.*)

Kids! Wow, you look great! How are you? How's the party? Yeah, Elton John's a good friend. Heavenly Mother invited me, but I guess she forgot to put my name on the list. But I really only came to see you guys. Brother St. Peter, could you ... uh ... could you leave us alone? Just for a few minutes. Thanks. 'Preciate ya.

(*St. Peter leaves.*)

How are Grandma Blossom and Grandma Butterfly? Good! And your mother? Great! Hey, I thought maybe sometime you guys could get a special day pass and come down and visit me. Your Grandpa Gerald is there, too, and all your other wicked relatives. It's really hot, but it just feels like another circuit party in Miami. Do you still know your Shakespeare? "Tomorrow and tomorrow and tomorrow ..." Terrific! Hey, I brought the ABBA CDs! I snuck them through the check-in. I thought they'd be a nice change from Afterglow. I know it's been tough. I'm sorry I was so ... human. I just hope you don't think you were a mistake or that I abandoned you. I brought you these! (*Holds up daffodils.*) I guess all I really wanted to say was hello ... and ... I love you.

Oh, my gosh! That's it! That's the password! Just four simple letters. "L-O-V-E." How could I forget? How could I be so stupid? I knew the password the whole time! Quick! Enter it in the computer before St. Peter gets back!

(*Disco ball goes and ABBA music plays "Angel Eyes." Steven steps on the carpet, but this time it does not burn his feet. Standing now inside the Pearly Gates as bubbles fall from Heaven.*)

Shall we dance?
(*After dancing with his children, Steven looks up and sees someone from his past*)

Jimmy!

(*Blackout.*)

Communications and Excommunications

MISSION CALL

Office of the First Presidency
Salt Lake City, Utah 84150

11 May 1989

Elder Steven Heard Fales
Vegas Verde, Las Vegas Nevada Lakes
4000 Paso De Oro
Las Vegas, Nevada 89102

Dear Elder Fales:

You are hereby called to serve as a missionary of The
Church of Jesus Christ of Latter-day Saints. You are assigned
to labor in the Portugal Porto Mission. It is anticipated that
you will serve for a period of 24 months.

You should report to the Missionary Training Center in
Provo, Utah, on Wednesday, 16 August 1989. You will learn the
discussions in Portuguese.

You have been recommended as one worthy to represent the Lord
as a minister of the restored gospel. You will be an official
representative of the Church. As such, you will be expected to
maintain highest standards of conduct and appearance by keeping
the commandments, living mission rules, and following the
counsel of your mission president.

You will also be expected to devote all your time and attention
to serving the Lord, leaving behind all other personal affairs.
As you do these things, the Lord will bless you and you will
become an effective advocate and messenger of the truth. We
place in you our confidence and pray that the Lord will help
you meet your responsibilities.

The Lord will reward the goodness of your life. Greater
blessings and more happiness than you have yet experienced
await you as you humbly and prayerfully serve the Lord in this
labor of love among his children.

We ask that you please send your written acceptance promptly,
endorsed by your bishop.

Sincerely,

President

EXCOMMUNICATION LETTER

THE CHURCH OF
JESUS CHRIST
OF LATTER-DAY SAINTS

SANDY UTAH CANYON VIEW STAKE

July 20, 2000

Steven Fales

Dear Brother Fales,

This letter will confirm the decision made at a Church disciplinary council held in your behalf on July 16, 2000, in the Sandy Utah Canyon View stake that you be excommunicated from the Church of Jesus Christ of Latter-day Saints for the practice of homosexuality. You should know that if you wish to appeal this decision that you may do so to the First Presidency through President Hunt.

Steven, we are most grateful that we had the opportunity to meet with you at this important meeting. Your honesty, openness, and the expression of your values and feelings were genuine and sincere. During that short time together we felt of your spirit and commend you for the devotion and dedication you have shown over your life to the Lord and His Church. We are saddened that your behavior has brought you to this point in your life.

Excommunication is the most severe Church disciplinary action. A person who is excommunicated is no longer a member of the Church. As such, you no longer have any privileges of Church membership. You may not wear temple garments or pay tithes and offerings. You may attend public Church meetings if your conduct is orderly, and we encourage you to do so. However, in such meetings you may not give a talk, offer a public prayer, partake of the sacrament, or participate in the sustaining of Church officers.

We realize you are going through a time of confusion in your life where many voices are pulling at you. We testify to you that the voice of truth is always manifested through the Holy Ghost. Until recently, this has been the voice you have faithfully followed. That voice is still available to you and will continue to manifest the Lord's plan of happiness to you if you will turn from your homosexual ways and follow the path of the Lord. You have the capacity to do this, Steven, and we pledge the support of your good bishop and our support in assisting you in this endeavor. The invitation of the Savior for you to come back to His Church is open to you. He will forgive you and make your life whole once again if you will repent and turn again to Him.

Steven Fales
Page 2
July 20, 2000

In the event you move from our stake, we are certain that your priesthood leaders in your new location would welcome the opportunity to get to know you and to be of assistance to you in your journey back into Church membership. If you will please keep in touch with Bishop ████████ or President ████ either one can connect you with your priesthood leaders regardless of where you may choose to live.

We express our love to you, Steven, and our support. We pray the Lord to bless you with personal strength and resolve throughout your repentance process.

Sincerely,

Sandy Utah Canyon View Stake Presidency

_____ _____ _____
████████████ ████████████ ████████████
President   First Counselor   Second Counselor

ON CRYSTAL METH

This is the actual email I mention in my play that I wrote coming down from my very first crystal meth binge. I hope to never do the drug again. Though much of this letter was the crystal talking (notice the length and thoroughness of some of the explanations!), it was the first time I realized that I had to stop escorting—for reasons I am only beginning to understand now. I hope the letter gives a bit of insight into the psychology of a sex worker hoping to transition. It is a letter written while in the depths of hell. If you have a problem with crystal meth or any other addiction . . . there is help. You don't have to do this alone.

New York City
Finished and sent Thursday, June 7, 2001, 11:18 A.M.

Dear S—,
Thank you for your emails and your call directing me to them. Email is so tricky. It is easily misunderstood and I want things to be clear between us. The last email I sent you was written in haste. I should have taken more time to carefully organize my thoughts and write with more clarity. You and our relationship deserved a much better email than the one I sent. There are many escorts who wouldn't think twice about losing a client and would not invest the entire night to write to you as I have done. But you very much deserve more than the typical client. I have written this with my heart. Please read it with yours.

Having re-read my recent email, I admit it comes across curt and flippant and does not give full resonance to the weight of what is at stake and the deep emotions at hand. I see it has made you angry. I hope this email will do you and myself justice. Know that this is my best attempt late into the night to explain how I see things and to apologize for any wrongs I have done or hurt I have caused. I'm sorry if it is too long, but I have some important things I need to say. Please forgive any spelling or grammatical errors I make. Especially forgive the parts that seem pedantic. As I am writing this, it is in many ways for me to clarify and organize and make sense of some things for myself. You are an educated, smart man and I don't mean to insult your intelligence or offend you in any way with my philosophizing, moralizing, or psycho-analyzing. Most of this I'm sure is bullshit. But I'm trying and trust you will glean what is true and what is a bit off, if not completely off-track, you will tolerate.

It is obvious that we both now realize the truth about our relationship. I admire you for coming to this truth clearly and so soon into our relationship. You are nipping it in the bud as you recognize that it won't work and it will save yourself even more pain, anger, resentment and money in the end. This is not a new realization. You came to it when you took me to dinner a few weeks ago. I think we both tried to brush it aside that night. You wanted this arrangement to work emotionally. I needed this arrangement to work financially. So we gave it another try, but the truth remains that ours could never be a truly committed loving relationship like I knew you wanted it to be because, essentially I was being paid to be in it and no amount would change the facts or my feelings in any lasting, significant way.

The other truth is that you gave and I took more than the relationship was worth. I helped lead you to believe that we could have much more than an arrangement or "paid" relationship. I knew from the beginning, though not as clearly as now, that this was impossible. I now see that I was unknowingly, but still responsible for, trying to keep a charade going. I didn't realize fully that I was playing it, but I certainly was. I must be accountable for my selfishness in keeping the charade going, which was not a caring or honest thing to do. I wanted to keep receiving your money and the generous gifts which you believed you were giving in return for a lasting, truly authentic loving relationship. One that you wanted, but which I knew could never be. You are no dumby. You started seeing things for what they were and are while I kept trying to keep the charade going when it was only going to hurt you. The relationship that you hoped for and wanted was never going to be the only one that I knew it could be.

One of the most trite but true statements in the world is that though you may be able to buy sex, you can't buy love or happiness. Escorts and all the rest of the pimps out there want you to believe you can get love ad happiness if you purchase the sex. You got hot sex, charm, and a smile from me, but then you mistakenly hoped if you paid enough it could grow into something resembling love and true caring and even fidelity. We wanted you to think that so you'd just buy more sex. But we knew the rest of the package would never come in the mail. I knew from the beginning that this was a false hope, but I didn't say a thing. I aided you in your own deception for my financial needs. You then invested more emotionally and financially than was in your best interests. You didn't get, and never would get what you wanted me to be. Unfortunately the buyer is not protected in this business. There is no money back guarantee and there are really no legal rights because prostitution is illegal anyway!

I understood why you feel so angry. You have every right to be. Like I said, you were taken advantage of by me (though not as methodically or maliciously as you may think). I did ultimately care more about subtley manipulating more and more money from you, than taking the high road and thinking of your true needs and very real feelings. I am capable of the high road and I sadly admit I chose the low. I feel badly about that because it hurt you. That is why I am not really cut out for this business. I'm not supposed to feel remorse for hurting or deceiving people. But I do.

It is such a simple fact of life really, that we have to sift through the false advertising and deceit when making a purchase. Buyer beware. Capitalism to some extent is built on this cut throat selling gimmick. Everyone is trying to sell you something. Often we buy it because we want or need it, but so often there were red flags and fine print we didn't take the time to read or examined and we get burned. Because we wasted our money on an imitation or wrong thing entirely. Sometimes we willingly forget this fact because we want something we don't have badly enough. When you told me you were falling in love with me, or getting near that point, I should have stopped everything right then and there. It would have solved most of the anger and pain you are experiencing now. But I didn't and I kept up appearances to make another sale.

One truth on the other side of the coin is that courtesans have no rights or security that they will get what they want. We can think we have a secure gig in a particular client, and may be told we will be loved and provided for indefinitely by that client, like in this case and many other great gigs I have seen blow away (especially a early client that liked to write me $5,000 checks! That promised me he would never abandon me! I was a fool to believe that lie.) the minute you think you have it in the bag, watch out. Your last incredible date/appointment that you thought would bring you the next (because you thought you kept him believing the illusion more than ever before) may very well be the last time you see him or his money again. Courtesans often have their own delusional thinking that causes them pain and lots of bounced checks! Believe it or not, some of us actually believe it is possible to find a life-long partner to love us in a client! There is no need to go into the faulty logic in that kind of thinking. It does not end in a happy union in the end.

I want to fully take my part in this drama by admitting that I always knew our relationship would ultimately go sour. I am a paid escort or courtesan (a male courtesan in this case). I know there are much harsher names for this, the oldest profession in the world, but please indulge my need to keep some sense of dignity. I have been selling an illusion of love and romance (thrown in with the illegal reality but expectation of sex) in exchange for money. Lot's of it. Having admitted that, I, and all courtesans, in our desire to have the security of repeat clients have only one real apology to make to our clients. We deliberately fail to inform or remind our clients that the illusion of our love (that they may or may not acquaint with sex) they are paying handsomely for is not real. Call it false advertising, plain lies and deceit or what you will. The courtesan does everything possible to keep the distinguished, wealthy client from believing, remembering, or admitting and sometimes even knowing to begin with that the magic in the magic show is just a trick. Anyone who hires courtesans is in more danger of forgetting the limits of the transaction whenever they start seeing one exclusively. In the end I knew that my feelings for you could never be what you hoped they were. Even up to my last email I was in one way or another, and not even meaning to really, trying to get you to believe the illusion.

As in sales of any kind and throughout history, customers are manipulated into buying so that someone, in this case the courtesan, can make money to live on (or it may seem in many contemporary courtesan cases today, to buy Prada). I think it is important to note that what the shrewd courtesan wants to assume is that the client purchasing the courtesan's time (and talents) is fully aware what the unstated agreement is. That when the hour paid for is over, so is the relationship. And any feelings the client has upon leaving that makes him feel the relationship means more to the courtesan than money, has been cast under her/his spell and will end up looking the fool.

The client is an audience member, not an actor like the courtesan. And like all audiences, they want to believe the illusion. They all too often mistakenly think they are the leading man in the scene. When this happens, they find they are really just the clown and get no final bow with the leading lady (or male escort in my case). Is it really the courtesan's right and responsibility to remind the client that he is not the leading man in the upcoming scenes but just the audience? Probably not. But when he is a genuinely good person, like you, I think the courtesan should watch out for him. But remember, to your credit, you caught on quickly and were not duped by the actor/courtesan Steven and prevented him from making you look like a clown.

Again, the relationship at times may seem real, but hiring a courtesan is much like watching a play on stage. The actors, the story, the whole production with scenery, props, lights, music and dance is an illusion for a paying audience of one. The fact, which has now been repeated far too many times, is that it is not real, but ENTERTAINMENT. What so often happens is that an emotional attachment muddies and blurs the lines, leading to heartbreak and a lot of money lost. At the end of every run of a show they strike the stage and nothing remains. The actors are now looking for new work and start rehearsals for an entirely new play. No run lasts forever. And no audience stays for every show. This is the great tradition that goes back for ages.

I failed to adequately remind you of the dead end you were coming to. I could see your jealously of my other clients. You thought some kind of open relationship would work. I knew it wouldn't. You said things about being honest, but I knew you had a difficult time knowing if I was out with for example, the Ambassador, so I wanted to protect you from the truth. You wanted loyalty and exclusivity so I tried to give you that illusion, and at the same time, you would be seeing people as well. There would always be a double standard. So it was a nice idea, but you have seen very quickly that it was impossible. And even if you could pay me enough to be your exclusive courtesan, I would always be a kept man with all the conflict and turmoil that would ultimately bring, especially if I fell in love with someone I wanted to be with. That ultimately would have happened.

I would never be what you wanted and for you to be what I wanted, a sugar daddy, would cost me a large piece of my truth and much freedom. Imagine how that multiplies when one has many sugar daddy's. I lose my freedom. I was to act like I loved you, even if I never said the words, but would never fully mean because my actions would betray me. To your credit and because you are very different from the others and much more handsome, I actually considered falling in love with you. But I couldn't, because, although you were my favorite client, you were still a client. And though I may have been your favorite escort, I was still an escort. That's just the way it is. And even if I tried to act the part of being your lover, I am not a very good actor in real life. Sooner or later my performances ring hollow. Especially with regards to my double life as an escort. I see already that both lives are blending into one and I'm afraid of what will become of me. Especially in regards to my relationships and the potential of a long-term relationship with another gay man. I'm afraid I will start playing my escort tricks and quoting lines that will affect my performance in the play I want to act well in more than any other.

I was overwhelmed with your generosity the first time we met through (agency). (What a tip! The biggest I had ever received!) How could I not be completely bedazzled at the possibility of getting so much for what seemed so little. But now I see that I have been a clown myself. I thought I could sell my affections and that they didn't mean that much to me. I now know that they are very dear to me and cost me every time I casually give them to strangers. It diminishes me and depletes me—and ultimately hurts my clients, like it has hurt you. I can't go on selling myself off. I fear I will be left with nothing, my spirit and my future happiness. I have been lying to myself, to you, and the others.

In addition to financial need, I have had an emotional need which gets met to some extent through escorting. That is a need for external praise that I am special and beautiful and talented and valued. Many of those needs are getting filled, I hope, now that I'm adjusting to life after divorce. But escorting is not the healthiest way to get these needs met. It all gets boiled down to getting paid for sex—and being objectified. I get paid for external beauty and charm but not for the real me. One small example is the way I have to hide behind my hairpieces. I know without it clients wouldn't say half of what they say nor would I have the success I have. As an escort you are always putting on a show. It's time to get real. As you see, I have these and many other things to deal with and sort out. I probably do need some therapy.

I started realizing these and other things last night when I saw the movie *Moulin Rouge*. I know I suggested we see it together, but I am very glad we did not have to sit through it side by side. It would have been torture for me AND for you. It called us on our faulty thinking regarding our relationship and helped me see many things about myself that I was denying. I think it is a beautiful film and we should both see it, but not together.

Moulin Rouge is the story of a Courtesan. I couldn't believe the irony as I watched the movie. It was painful and jolting to watch so much of my life and problems and our current situation being paralleled on the screen. When you see the movie, this will make much more sense. Just like the courtesan Nicole Kidman plays, I have justified prostituting myself for the dream of becoming a great actor. (How perfect that you just wrote that you wondered about this "escort/actor thing!" It is a thing to be wondering about!)

I left the movie with my thoughts and emotions spinning in my head and my denials vanishing into the bleak truth of what I have become and thinking what I must do to change. The reality that was starting to dawn on me made for a very slow walk home that lead me to a very dark, depressing, and terrible night and day which I do not care to go into or repeat again. When I finally returned home late this evening (I did not come home last night), your well-timed emails should have come as no surprise. All this lead to this reality: *I must stop escorting or it will destroy me and any possibility of the future I truly want for myself, and in some way that I don't fully understand, for my children.* It compromises my true desires and feelings and takes away my freedom to be the man I truly know I am deep inside. The irony again is that I sacrificed so much, my church membership and my marriage, to be what I know to be an authentic part of myself. I cannot continue to discredit this triumph I hold so dear by continuing to be fake in ways that escorting continues to enforce in me. I must stop now before things get out of hand. Which is already starting to happen. I hope it is not too late. I like to think my stint of escorting was a necessary evil that helped to get me on my feet. Remember, I moved to this impossible, ridiculously expensive, yet necessary-to-be-here city sixty thousand dollars in debt and with sixty dollars in my pocket. I had no one, not even well to do parents, willing to help me get set up and make my career, dreams, and new life happen. Not to mention I had no idea when I would see my dear children again because there was no way I could afford a plane ticket back to see them for what would be months and months. I barely had a week's money to eat or ride the subway with, let alone get new headshot's printed and pay for telephone calls to talk to my kids in Utah. Escorting seemed the best and easiest way out at the time. It hit me as an idea out of the blue. I didn't know a thing about it or how to do it. All I knew was that it would provide financial freedom so I would have the time, energy, and means to focus on and make my acting career happen AND to help provide for my children and see them on a monthly basis. And it has seemed to do the trick up until now.

In the last six months, and in no small part because of you, I have exceeded my original expectations regarding the money escorting would make me. In addition to all the money, I have shopped, dined, slept, socialized with incredibly wealthy and powerful men at some of the finest stores, restaurants, hotels, penthouses, theatres and concert halls in the world. I've lived like a prince (or a courtesan!) going wherever and doing and buying essentially whatever I needed and wanted! I have been showered with gifts and praise and adoration here in the most amazing city in the world. To my surprise I found that I am a damn good escort, if not exceptional. Far better than most in looks, charm, intelligence, humor, style, and yes sexual technique. I could make quite a very lucrative career of it for years to come, due in no small part to my youthful face and those handy, expensive hairpieces (the escorting paid for!). So though I am thirty-one and my hair is thinning, with my face, fake hair and the help of a personal trainer (which again escorting has paid for with an occasional facial or two to boot), I can easily compete with the many young, handsome escorts desired and routinely hired by that disconcerting number of wealthy gay men in this city for quite a few years to come. Most of these men, like you, have been complete gentlemen. Since I first came to New York in January and immediately started working as an escort (in addition to waiting tables mind you), I have seen and experienced some of the most fabulous things in the past six months that would take others from my social class and Mormon background six years, if not a lifetime, if at all, to encounter. In many ways this education in the ways of the world has been a blessing, in others, a curse. I am not quite the bubbly, optimistic young actor I first was when I got here. In some ways it serves me, but at the same time I can tell I am developing an edge that is not always a pretty thing and must monitor before it makes me bitter and jaded like so many here in NYC.

I am pleased to report that most of the money I have made escorting has been used for the purpose for which it was originally intended: paying off debts, launching my acting/writing career, traveling monthly to Utah to see my children, paying child support, and getting set up in one of the most expensive and toughest cities in the world. I found I occasionally had the money to help family members and friends in need and would give generously. And yet I must also confess, some of the money I've spent selfishly on clothes, parties, and frivolous items I bought to nurture myself and help me feel like I actually am worth a few nice things. Perhaps I did this to counteract the internalized shame and self-criticism I often feel (and have felt from many in my family and the Mormon sub-culture that didn't appreciate and support me as a gay man) in failing in my efforts to be straight and my recent divorce and excommunication. Time will tell if this escorting holiday I have taken from reality was worth the potential costs. I don't know the answer. I just pray, in the name of *Moulin Rouge* and all that is holy, I don't have some undetected, incurable illness waiting to take me from my full potential and my children before I get to find out.

It is uncomfortably clear that when I stop escorting, life will be harder financially, but I know I am capable of making money legitimately. Escorting has spoiled me to some degree and threatened my work ethic, but I have worked hard in the past and can do it again. I believe life will be happier and more authentic and free when I do things the old-fashioned way and not take short cuts. And who knows, maybe my acting career will take me to the financial and artistic heights, that before I became sidetracked, I'd been working so hard for years to achieve. If not, there's bound to be something that with my master's degree and charisma (and let's not forget humility) can do.

This letter is now far too long. I started it Wednesday night and it is now 11:00 A.M. Thursday morning. I have not slept now in 48 hours so I admit this attempt to be clear is now muddied in confusion.

I would like to think I am wrong, but I believe in the future I will end up paying harsh, previously unexamined consequences for choosing to escort. An obvious dilemma is if anyone finds out about it. As of yet, not a single family member, friend, or industry professional knows that I have essentially been a prostitute. I don't believe anyone can judge me for what I have done, but if it does ever get out, I will have to deal with the shame it could bring to my children and my family, and the possible effects the stigma would have on my acting career. What is at the bottom of this lengthy letter, which I fear has become a vague and masturbatory, is that I admit that I have hurt you, and that I am sorry. I can see that I will pay a price for this. I will lose a dear, wonderful, generous, loving, supportive man's friendship and confidence. It has already happened. You are right in what you wrote tonight. It is not possible for us to just be friends now. There is too much pain and loss. But as any objective, outside party can see, we have at least both honorably fulfilled our ends of the bargain. I have performed, at least for a time, a role for you. You have paid the actor's fee. The show, though beautifully presented (or not so beautifully presented—if not acted downright appallingly), is over.

You have already admitted your share of the blame for this charade. I hope I have now fairly acknowledged mine so the scales are balanced and that you don't feel angry at me. It is my wish that we part in peace. I want you to know and believe, because it is the truth, that I do care about you. You have done so many wonderful things for me and my children. I will never forget your kindness. You HAVE been a godsend and have helped me so much on this challenging, confusing, and terrifying journey I am on. You have given so much of your time, talent, love, not to mention money. Thank you for rooting for me. I think you know deep down I have genuinely given something of my best self to you. At least a bit more caring, I hope, than your average boy from (agency). Because I do care about you, S—. Though the rules of the courtesan say this was a business transaction and that we escorts should lock our hearts and forsake emotions when it comes to getting involved with a client. Though it is in both of our best interests to now part ways and move on with our lives without regular contact, if any, I know in my heart that we both gave a little bit if not a lot more than was required. I hope you agree and that you won't regret the investment you made in this relationship and that you will remember the good times we've shared. Our paths collided here in New York for a reason. (Even if it was to help me see that I need to get out of escorting and that you better not hire one ever again!) There are no accidents. Thanks for teaching me many important things. I am so glad I got to know you, S—.

I want you to know that if I can someday be of any help to you in anyway, it would be my pleasure to do something to pay you back for your kindness. Or just to do something for a wonderful person and a dear old friend. So don't hesitate to let me know. You have my numbers and if I'm ever famous, just call my agent! One important decision I have made for both of us, if you haven't already come to it yourself: I will not be accepting any more money or gifts of any kind from you. It is not right for me to expect anything more, nor would it be appropriate for you to give it. It would be taking advantage of you for me to ask. And the reality is that I am and will be fine. Spend your money on those who will be able to freely return your love and affection. Whoever they are now or will be in the future, they are very lucky.

Please dissolve the trust fund you set up for my children.

The one loose end is the mobile phone. I don't know what kind of long-term contract they had you sign so I don't know if it is possible to discontinue the service on it without a penalty, but paying the penalty might be the easiest way to go. I would like to keep the phone, if that is okay, and at a later date, when I am ready, I will purchase my own plan and get a new number. It is not essential that I have a mobile phone right now. I've got my service number which is all I need for now.

So in closing . . . I don't think it is a good idea for us to see each other now for quite a while. Oh, I'm sure we're bound to run into each other sooner than later, but for now, we need a major time out. Just throw that terrible, stupid toothbrush away and keep the pictures you took of me in some envelope in your desk if you decide not to burn them which you better not! We are both now free. I don't think we need to talk this through. Just let me know in an email what we should do about the phone and I will trust that you are well and happy and vice versa.

I wish you the best and hope you have taken this letter in the spirit it was written in. Again, I apologize for any condescending tone or poor wording in this or the previous emails that may have offended you or made you angry.

With admiration and appreciation,
Steven Fales

P.S. It IS, however, okay for ME to give YOU one last gift. It is small. Just a token. I have received much from you. You don't have anything really from me. I would like to give you something and will send it in the mail. (*It was the soundtrack to* Moulin Rouge.)

This client told me he spent over $80,000 on me. He eventually lost his job and Upper East Side apartment after a long relapse on alcohol. We talk about once a year. As of this writing, he is doing well in recovery and lives in Florida. He became a friend and helped me transition financially out of the business, for which I will always be grateful.

About Nudity

There was almost more drama getting the show mounted than in the play itself.

Confessions of a Mormon Boy was originally supposed to open Off-Broadway at the new Acorn Theatre on Forty-second Street the summer of 2003. It obviously didn't.

I had done a workshop run of my solo play at the Jose Quintero Theatre on Forty-second Street in June 2002 to get the piece ready for a run in San Francisco. Several producers came and showed interest in making a commercial run in New York happen. I decided to go with the veteran Broadway producers who had the biggest and flashiest office, of course. They said all the right things, telling me that the play had universal themes and that they felt it really had cross-over potential. When they told me some of the hit plays they had produced in the past, I was star-struck.

I couldn't believe this was my life!

They arranged for me to meet Jack Hofsiss in his Upper West Side apartment. I performed for him right there in his living room—pressing "play" myself for the most important sound cues in the show. His Tony Award for *The Elephant Man* was sitting next to him on the table. It was more impressive and intimidating to me than any Oscar. I was ecstatic when Jack agreed to direct the piece.

When I told them I wanted to tell my whole story, they were very enthusiastic. I wrote a new version, putting the escorting and drug use in (as well as the new reveal at the end). They flew out with Jack to Salt Lake City where I was going to be trying out the new material. (This was a very different version than Salt Lake City had seen a year before!) They casually mentioned after seeing it that they thought it needed nudity. I blew it off. They couldn't be serious. They also suggested I change the title. They agreed that *X'd: Confessions of a Mormon Boy* would do. ("X'd" for excommunicated.)

They arranged a week-long writing workshop with Jack Hofsiss in New York. Together he helped me shape the piece further. Jack would listen and ask me questions. (Jack has an amazing ear for language and truthfulness—and he helped me edit my narcissism out, if that is even possible.) We would work together, then I would go to my room at the Mayflower hotel and write. No playing. No partying. Then we'd get back together the next day. Sometimes he would want to cut something I thought should stay. I would try it out. Sometimes it would work. And sometimes he'd say, "Yes, put it back in." We had a wonderful ebb and flow as we honed the piece.

I learned so much about writing in that one week working with this world-class theatre artist. Jack was the perfect director for this show. He understood the longing for reconciliation with religion as a gay Catholic. He was sensitive to that. He also knew about choosing not to be a victim. He has been paralyzed from the waist down since his tragic accident in the 80s. He continued to direct on and off Broadway from his wheelchair.

At the last minute, the producers arranged to do a 10-week run at the Coconut Grove Playhouse in Miami under Jack's direction to get it ready for the Off-Broadway run. It was a critical and popular success, breaking box office expectations. We were ready for New York.

I went home to Utah to spend time with my mom and my kids and prepare for my big break.

☙

Just days before I was to fly to Salt Lake to begin rehearsals, I got a call from the lead producer telling me not to get on the JetBlue flight. I was told that their main "mystery" investor had fallen through.

It felt like I'd been hit by a truck. How could this be? Hadn't I raised one-fourth of the budget for the commercial run myself? How could we have sent the press release out to the world when we didn't have the money?! (I learned later that producers do this all the time. There's a reason Broadway is called the "Fabulous Invalid"!)

The producers told me not to worry. The show was being bumped until the fall. Postponed is different than cancelled. So I took heart. Regardless, I sank into a depression for about a month. I was completely broke, camping out at my mom's place in god-forsaken southern Utah (where you rub shoulders with polygamist wives at Wal-mart) until my ship came in. I had child support to pay and now no job. I had been paid a small royalty advance, but the money was long gone. I spent my time working on new material. When I get depressed, I write and work harder.

Then a call finally came from the producers.

I was asked to consider getting completely naked in the play. During the costume change half-way through the show, I was to get down to authentic-looking Mormon undergarments and then get full-frontal nude before putting on the black 2(ˣ)ist underwear. Like I said, this had been suggested to me a year before when the producers had come to Salt Lake City. I had thought the request was a joke. I was hoping it was a joke.

There was no way I could use Mormon undergarments in the show. I may be excommunicated, but I was not a Son of Perdition! When I saw Joe Pitt in *Angels in America: Perestroika* take his garments off onstage I was totally offended. Garments are the most sacred article of worship in Mormonism. I could talk about them, but using them onstage would be going too far. I had to have some respect. I couldn't use the real thing. I felt using conservative white boxers over my black briefs would be a good compromise.

Hadn't the play been doing just fine without nudity?

I was told that we could get the final investors we needed if I complied. When nudity is added in "gay plays", you get the initial gay ticket coming just for the nudity alone. Recoupment is often possible just because of the nudity. Hadn't I seen Nicole Kidman myself in *The Blue Room* on Broadway? It didn't do anything for me, but I sure did see the house filled! And I have to admit, I saw Ronnie Larsen's *Making Porn* in San Diego starring Falcon lifetime exclusive adult porn-star Matthew Rush. Though the artwork for the show might look like we were *Making Porn*, this play was anything but.

I was told that the nudity could be quick and that the lighting could be suggestive and shadowy. But I could just see myself in the situation where subtle lighting in rehearsal could turn to a spotlight in previews. From the tone in the producer's voice, I could tell this my choice was either going to launch the off-Broadway run or be a deal-breaker.

I couldn't believe this was my life!

So I asked every veteran theatre professional I knew what they thought. It was a unanimous consensus that if I added nudity it would ruin my show. Sometimes nudity is necessary and adds to the story. Sometimes it doesn't.

I even did a benefit staged reading for the Desert AIDS Project in Palm Springs and asked the entire room at the end if the play warranted nudity. What I got was a resounding no from the room packed with gay men.

So I wrote a very respectful letter to the producers explaining why I wouldn't be able to honor their request.

First of all, I was a recovering sex-worker. If I were to get fully-naked onstage in my play, I felt it would discount the message of the show, undermining the integrity of the piece and leaving the audience questioning my intentions to get onstage in the first place. Wasn't the play about getting naked by taking the hairpiece off, not my underwear?

I had made a commitment only a year and a half before to never escort again. I felt if I got naked onstage (for me!) I would be releasing an addiction all over again. I was still in the process of de-toxing from "working it." I might as well start dancing at the Gaeity at Times Square. (Not that there's anything wrong with that!)

I was also thinking about my kids. No, daddy wasn't going to be getting naked onstage. It just didn't feel appropriate. Sorry to seem like a prude, but when you have children, you start to see the world differently. You are not as quick to just do whatever you want (believe it or not!).

Part of the gimmick/hook of the show was to look like I could still escort—and still choose to not. (It's hard work keeping the "boy" in *Mormon Boy!*) I felt that I was giving the audience sufficient eye-candy by getting down to the black underwear. I was getting my exhibitionist jollies off already—without having to take such a giant step back. Not to mention, I'm a grower, not a show-er!

I also felt that artistically it was more sexy not to show it all. And classier and more elegant. This was a form of simple story telling—the direction was minimalist as well. We'd let language and suggestion be enough. We'd leave it up to imagination. Isn't that theatre? Shakespeare had done that quite effectively, right? And the Greeks never showed nudity or violence onstage. And this wasn't the '70s where we needed nudity onstage for nudity's sake.

And I didn't want to offend the audience I wanted most to see my work. If there was nudity, many would not come. That was another reason swearing was practically non-existent in the piece. Like I said the artwork was risqué enough. And the "Lizard scene" and the "escort montage" were PG-13 at least! Getting naked, in my mind, would limit the possibility of the show crossing over.

I told them also, that at the very end of my play, I declare with all the energy of my soul that, "I'm getting my integrity back. And my life is starting to work. And it makes me smile. *Really* smile. And I wouldn't jeopardize that for all the *foie gras* in the world." I would not be able to smile or feel proud of this play if I took all my clothes off. I was already exposing myself on levels that go far above and beyond the call of duty.

This show was my prayer. I would not be able to offer it, nor would it ascend, if I compromised on this matter.

So after I sent them the letter (four drafts!) I got a call. The lead producer said that they wanted me to carefully reconsider. When I said that I wouldn't, they said they would have to reconsider doing my play at all. The conversation ended.

A month went by. I got a call telling me that they would not be doing the play. I asked for the rights back. They said no because I didn't seem grateful enough for all they had done for the project. They didn't like my tone. I guess I couldn't keep up the Mormon charm when my integrity was at stake.

I had to wait another four months for the option to expire. I had to wait to get the rights back to my own show about my life.

This *was* my life!

When I got the rights I decided to change the title back and asked Jack if he would stay with the project, which he was happy to do. I applied to the New York International Fringe Festival and we got in at the last minute. We became a breakout hit.

Though many producers came, I felt the piece was so personal I needed to produce it myself—for better or for worse.

I really lucked out when I met a cracker-jack young (straight) producer and general manager named Seth Goldstein of The Splinter Group. He was young and ambitious and tenacious. We were a perfect team. And together we pulled off the impossible: We raised the money. We hand-picked a team that really felt passionately about the play. We did the show as a fundraiser at the Mitzi Newhouse Theatre at Lincoln Center for The Point Foundation. (The Mormon Temple towering across the street!) We got Jack Hofsiss into the SoHo Playhouse (which is not wheelchair accessible due to it's Landmark Building status) using a special wheelchair lift he discovered! We had meeting after meeting in the TDF Conference Room across from his office. We even took time to dine at The Spotted Pig. It was a magical time producing the off-Broadway run together all while I was doing eight shows a week. I couldn't have done it without him and his team. We could devote an entire chapter to this book with the adventures we had together.

Everything happens for a reason. In many ways, I should thank those producers. I learned many things about producing from them. And the postponement gave me time to catch up to my writing. I had mapped out my healing cerebrally, but there is nothing like Time to season us and make us stronger—to give us peace and perspective. And above all, it allowed me to spend important quality time with my kids that I otherwise would have sacrificed had everything happened earlier in New York.

I am learning to stop needing to please everyone. I am learning to trust myself. And I am learning to trust in the process. As Viola says in *Twelfth Night*, "O time, thou must untangle this, not I; It is too hard a knot for me to untie."

Resources

The following are resources related to themes in *Confessions of a Mormon Boy*:

QUEER SPIRITUALITY

Affirmation (GLBT Mormons) : www.affirmation.org
Reconciliation (Gay Mormons): www.ldsreconciliation.org
Integrity (Gay Episcopalians): www.integrityusa.org
Dignity (Gay Catholics): www.dignityusa.org
Seventh-day Adventist Kinship (Gay SDA): www.sdakinship.org
Gay Jehovah's Witnesses: www.gayxjw.org
Gay Jews: www.gayjews.com
Q-Spirit: www.qspirit.org
Soulforce: www.soulforce.org

FAMILY

Straight Spouse Network: www.ssnetwk.org
Children of Gays and Lesbians: www.colage.org
Family Pride: www.familypride.org
Gay & Bi Fathers' Forum of NYC: www.gaybidads.org
Gamofites (Gay Mormon Fathers): www.gamofites.org
P-Flag: www.pflag.org
Family Fellowship: www.ldsfamilyfellowship.org
Wildflowers Foundation (co-founded by ex-wife Emily Pearson):
www.wearewildflowers.com

RECOVERY

Many addicts have found help in 12-step programs such as:

Alcoholics Anonymous (AA): www.alcoholics-anonymous.org
Crystal Meth Anonymous (CMA): www.crystalmeth.org
Sex Workers Anonymous (SWA): www.sexworkersanonymous.com
Sexual Compulsives Anonymous (SCA): www.sca-recovery.org
Sex and Love Addicts Anonymous (SLAA): www.slaafws.org
Debtors Anonymous (DA): www.debtorsanonymous.org

Other:
www.lifeormeth.com
www.gaymeth.org
GMHC (Gay Men's Health Crisis): www.gmhc.org

Possibilities:
Possibilities is a proposed new organization that provides education and resources to assist sex workers desiring to transition out of the sex industry. To find out more about how you can helpmake this organization possible, contact Steven Fales at escortsnomore@aol.com.

MISCELLANEOUS

Landmark Education ("The Forum"): www.landmarkeducation.com

Official Web site of The Church of Jesus Christ of Latter-day Saints: www.lds.org or www.mormons.org

National Association of Research and Therapy of Homosexuality www.narth.org

Focus on the Family: www.family.org *or* www.exodus.to

Exodus International: www.exodus.to
Evergreen International: www.evergreeninternational.org

Mormon Alliance:
www.mormonalliance.org *or* www.lds-mormon.com

Sunstone Symposium: www.sunstoneonline.com

Human Rights Campaign: www.hrc.com

Alfieri Salon: www.alfieri.com

Books by Carol Lynn Pearson, author of *Good-bye, I Love You*
www.clpearson.com

Mormon Boy: www.mormonboy.com
This is the home of *Confessions of a Mormon Boy* and Mormon Boy
Productions, LLC.

"Because I'm not a boy. I'm a man. And I'm a dad." *(Carol Rosegg)*

One Final Confession

Some people have a bad hair day once in a while. I've had a bad hair life.

Was it the clippers mom always used on my fine hair? Was it that I always blow dried it, feathered it, and then lacquered it with Aqua Net? Was it that I tried to turn it blonde with peroxide as a teenager? Was it that I would curl it with a curling iron my senior year of high school? I've had more hair styles than Hillary Clinton!

The best hair I ever had was my freshman year of college at the Boston Conservatory. But as soon as I started my Mormon mission to Portugal, my hair started to thin.

Finally in the middle of grad school I got hair transplants to try to salvage what I had left. But that was a miserable, painful, expensive process that yielded very poor results. (It's not a good idea to use student loan money for elective surgery.) And Rogaine and Propecia would never give me the density I wanted.

My mom had quite a collection of wigs growing up, so I got the hairpiece idea (and my fine hair) from her. (Even my dad has more hair than me!)

The third and last year of grad school I took my casting type into my own hands and invested in a hair system. The results were incredible. Nothing compares to the density of a good hair piece. The key is in styling it well. I prefer a Caesar cut and use lots of gel so it blends into my real hair on the sides. Toupee clips are the way to go. No need to bond it on with glue. It just clips right on to the little hair I have left. And the pieces can last a long time—just needing a little color here and there.

I got new headshots taken and started using the hairpieces at auditions. I finally had the leading man hair I always wanted. And even the most jaded agents couldn't tell my hair was fake—or so they said. But, to my surprise, many theater companies preferred me without the hairpiece once they discovered they had an option.

When I got divorced, I started using my hairpieces at the bars. And then started using them for things *other* than auditions. Before I knew it, I was a slave to my hair. It just may be the biggest addiction I have. (It's also a nightmare trying to keep the "hair system" a secret during sex!)

So when I decided to take the darn thing off and threw it up in the air at that "course" I mention in the play, it was one of the most liberating, authentic experiences of my life.

The room of 500 people leapt to their feet. (And two men were so inspired that they came up to me and asked me if I knew of any groups that could help them stop doing sex-work. It was the beginning of my calling to try to help as many as I could avoid the pitfalls of the sex industry.) So I decided to re-create that moment on stage in an effort to help others find authenticity.

So now I take my hair off onstage all the time. I'm often told I'm better looking without the piece. In fact, when I first came home with the piece on, my son said, "I hate it!" Emily never liked it either.

But until I finish this project, at least, I wear my hair in public so as not to give away the surprise. But if you see me at the gym, I usually have a baseball cap on. If you see me at home, I'm running around without it.

Any guy I date has to like me for me, not my wig (or my rat, as I like to call it.)

There is a good chance that when I stop doing *Mormon Boy*, I will stop wearing a hairpiece and will just shave all my hair off. But I'm not promising anything.

And if you must get a hairpiece, I get mine from Alfieri Salon on Fifth Avenue in New York. Tell them I sent you! But if I ever find out you are using them to escort, I will track you down and rip the thing off myself!

Acknowledgments

It has taken a village. I have lived my "Mormon Boy" dream by the grace of God, friends, family, and colleagues. From sleeping on couches to getting rides to meals to buying tickets to the show and ultimately investing in my work, I owe so much to so many for this opportunity to have lived out of my suitcase!

First and foremost, thanks must be given to Emily Pearson and Carol Lynn Pearson for their feedback and contributions to the play and for signing depiction releases for themselves and for the children. And a very special thanks to my parents for being such good sports about my work and for loving me so unconditionally.

Thanks to Jack Hofsiss; Dan Wootherspoon and the Sunstone Institute; Roger Benington; Stephen Rosenfield and the American Comedy Institute; the staff at the Rose Wagner Performing Arts Center in Salt Lake City; Laina Thomas; the Hollywood Theatre in Portland, Oregon; Matthew Corrozine; Ed Decker and the staff at New Conservatory Theatre Center in San Francisco for taking a risk on an unknown solo artist; Ken Billington; Jack Hofsiss; Leonard Soloway; Steven Levy; Jack Hofsiss; Ken Daigle; Maureen; Arnold Mittelman and the staff at Coconut Grove Playhouse in Miami; Dan Kirsch and staff at Diversionary Theatre in San Diego; Dave Zak and the staff at Bailiwick Repertory Theatre in Chicago; Elena Holy and all my friends at the New York International Fringe Festival; Frank Mack and Connecticut Repertory Theatre; my many teachers at Boston Conservatory, BYU, UNLV, and UConn; Louis Burke; Moises Kaufman and his partner Jeff; Richard-Jay Alexander; Holly Villaire; David Alan Stern; Adam Muller; The Point Foundation and staff at Lincoln Center; Darren Cole; Faith Mulvehill, and Gabe at the Soho Playhouse; Jeremy Schaeffer, Chuck Mirarchi, Sam Rudy; Dale Heller; Clive Romney; Tim Saternow; Ellis Tillman; Rob Kaplovitz; Dorothy Shi;

Charles M. Turner III; Heather Hill; Mark Sendroff; Lee Beckstead; David and Carlie Hardy and family; Carl and Sharon Spaulding and family; Reed Cowan; Allen Burch; Patrick Mundt; Frank Matheson; Ray Gast; Brian Malk; Nancy Heitel; Harvey S. Shipley Miller; Barbara Hogeneson; Terry Bean; James and Lyndi Fales; Kyle and Julie Kimoto; Esther Paul; Joann Clark; Greg Wood; Richard Glazer; Gordon Wahl; Tom Seig, Chris Dobrusky; Chuck Dalke-Butler; Joseph Dalby; Boaz Dalit; Michael Rupert; Steven Wozencraft; Dick Data; Brondi Borer; Anne Decker; Jay Deratany; Emmett Foster; Russ Goringe; Robb Anderson; Bob Duva; Richard Levine; Brent Tingey; Jason Firth; BJ Engler; Bert Estrada; Nancy Thorup; Donald and Susie Wright; Lizz Parsons; John Andersen; Ira Gilbert; Jared Ivie; Steve and Linda Parkin; Douglas Sills; Sophie McLean, David Cunningham and others at Landmark Education; Lucie Arnaz; Nafe Katter; Stephen Johnson; Andrew Harvey; Ken Burman and Paul Gauntt; Lorna Kelly; Julie and Wade Forsythe; Polly Howell; Christopher Borg and the Mormon Boyz; Affirmation and Gamofites; Joe Pittman; Richard Fumosa; Ming Russell; William Gladstone; Seth and Molly Goldstein; and, the "Fellowship."

About the Playwright

Steven Fales was born in Provo, Utah, and began performing as a young boy singing solos in church. When his family later moved to Las Vegas, he started performing with his high school choir at Caesar's Palace and other major resorts on the Las Vegas strip. He trained on scholarship at the Boston Conservatory before serving a two-year mission to Portugal for the LDS Church. He then transferred to Brigham Young University where he completed his B.F.A. in musical theatre and later received an M.F.A. in acting from the University of Connecticut. Fales has performed at major Shakespeare festivals and regional theatre across the country. He is a sought after public speaker and writes a monthly column, "Ask Mormon Boy." Fales is currently working on a new solo-show called Mormon American Princess as he continues to perform *Confessions of a Mormon Boy* across the country. He has used his play to raise tens of thousands of dollars for charity. He lives in Salt Lake City, where he takes an active role in raising his two children, and can be reached at www.mormonboy.com.